Outback Sky

ANNIE SEATON

The Augathella Girls: Book 2

ANNIE SEATON

Dedication

For my armchair travelling readers.

ANNIE SEATON

The Augathella Girls series.

Book 1: Outback Roads – The Nanny

Book 2:Outback Sky – The Pilot

Book 3: Outback Escape – The Sister

Book 4: Outback Winds – The Jillaroo

Book 5: Outback Dawn – The Visitor

Book 6: Outback Moonlight – The Rogue

Book 7: Outback Dust – The Drifter

Book 8: Outback Hope – The Farmer

Augathella Characters-Book 2

Fallon Malone	Contract Pilot
Jon Ingram	Station Manager
George Malone	Fallon's great-uncle
Callie Young	Schoolteacher/ nanny
Braden Cartwright	Owner of Kilcoy Station
Rory, Nigel and Petie	Braden's sons
Sophie Cartwright	Braden's sister
Kent Mason	Owner of Lara Waters
Kimberley Riordan	School deputy principal
Bob Hamblin	School principal
Cheryl Hamblin	His wife
Jim Anderson	Local garage owner
Jennifer Shaw	School Counsellor

Chapter 1

The red, vintage F100 ute creaked when Fallon Malone leaned back and rested her elbows against the dusty bull bar. It was going to be a while before Jason arrived in the company helicopter so she put her head back, enjoying the morning sun on her face. There hadn't been much time for relaxation since she'd left Kununurra three weeks ago. The upcoming muster in an unfamiliar area and the state of Great-Uncle George's house had taken over her waking thoughts.

'It's only a little tidy-up, sweetie,' Mum had said when Fallon had mentioned she was going out Augathella way for a muster. 'Seeing you're going there, there's no point your father taking time off work and us driving all that way. Plus, you've got your ute if there's anything worth salvaging.'

Fallon shook her head as she thought back to that comment. That should have sent warning bells ringing. Anyway, her ute had gone in for a service when she'd hit town and needed major work done, so here she was, driving Uncle George's 1962 F100 ute. The ute was probably worth more than his house and its entire contents.

'And while you're there you can check poor Uncle George is eating properly. You're a good girl, Fallon. You appreciate the importance of family.'

After a restless night listening to creatures scurrying in the dark, Fallon had had enough of the house. She'd made herself a coffee in the grimy kitchen this morning dismissing the idea of a takeaway from the café; she didn't want to interact with people.

Yet.

Simply being away from the north and the black feeling that came with being up there was a relief, and she was determined to make the most of the time being away from memories.

The early morning sun bathed her face; it was nice out here at the Augathella Aerodrome. Soon, it would be too hot in the outback sun and she'd move into the shade. Hopefully, she wouldn't be at the airfield too long, although the alternative—sorting out a houseful of junk—was not appealing. The mountains in the distance held a pretty blue tinge as the sun climbed higher. The fresh air and the sunshine improved her mood and there was no one pressuring her. No one watching her every move. Fallon closed her eyes and tried to push away the thoughts of the north, but the image that replaced her memories was no better. She had to get that damn house out of her mind. Why the hell she'd

8

ever agreed to sort it out was beyond her. Her focus out here should be the muster, not huge piles of junk in a ramshackle old house.

'You never know, Uncle George might even leave it to you,' Mum had said when she'd called her parents from the garage to let them know she'd arrived safely.

Almost thirty and she still felt as though she had to do that. But ever since *the incident*, Mum had insisted.

The incident. These days she looked at her life as before and after. Maybe she should change careers but Fallon knew—and wanted to do— nothing else.

'A house out in the sticks?' she'd quickly answered. 'No, thanks, Mum. I don't want it and I certainly don't want the multitude of "treasures" inside.'

Despite working in the outback, Fallon spent most of her time up in North Queensland on the water when she wasn't flying. Last long break, she'd gone sailing in a hire yacht out of Cairns. Being in the air and on the water were her two favourite activities.

For the fifth time since she'd woken up this morning, she'd wondered how she'd got roped into this family chore.

'Why don't you and Dad come out and visit while I'm here? If Dad's busy, you could catch a bus, I'm sure there'd be one from Brisbane.'

'I'd love to, Fal, but I've got the Red Cross fete to organise, and then we've got the cake stall. I couldn't possibly get away . . . maybe if Augathella was closer . . .'

'Stop thinking about it,' Fallon told herself. 'You cannot afford to get stressed out here.' She'd had her fair share of stress, and she rolled her eyes as she picked at a piece of skin at the side of her thumbnail.

Her stress indicator: chewed fingernails and ragged skin. She shoved her hands into her jeans pockets and vowed she'd leave them alone from now on.

'It's only just a little tidy up, love, before he sells the place and goes into the aged care home. We have to remember he's getting on.'

'How old is Uncle George anyway? I thought he was ancient when we came out here when I was a kid.'

'He's fifteen years older than my mum, so he must be about ninety now. But don't worry, he's as sharp as a tack. I just worry that no one checks on his physical well-being. So, seeing you're out there . . .'

Fallon sighed. 'So, what sort of a "little" tidy up?' she asked, reluctantly giving in.

'Apparently, he's sold most of the land, and his little house on the edge of town just needs to be cleaned up. You know, just sort the house for him, mow the lawn, tidy the gardens up ready to put it on the market. Maybe you could live there while you're doing the contract work.'

'And when does he want to move out?'

'He told me a couple of weeks ago he's got an independent living unit reserved at the aged care home in town. He's keen to sell the house so he can move across to it. The poor dear sounds more than ready.'

So, Fallon had rolled into town with a troubled gearbox, deposited her car at the local garage to have it looked at, called her parents, and then asked for directions to George Mason's house, hoping there was a spare bed there for her.

'It's on the edge of town, isn't it?' she'd asked the man at Andersen's garage.

'Don't tell me you're looking to buy that house?' He'd scratched his head and frowned at her. 'Needs a bit of work.'

'No, I'm going to visit George,' she replied.

'He's not there,' came the quick reply.

For one moment, she worried that Great-Uncle George had gone on to a better place. 'He's not there?' she repeated slowly.

'No, love. The council threatened to condemn his house, so he chucked a wobbly, and moved into the aged care home up the road there.'

'Chucked a wobbly?'

'Yeah, you know. Had a dummy spit. George is renowned for that. Sorry, if you're a rellie, I shouldn't be critical.'

Fallon waved her hand. 'Don't worry about that. I only met him once a long time ago. Anyway, how long do you think my ute will take to get fixed?'

'Love, by the sound of that gearbox, I think it'll be in here at least ten days. I have to get parts sent down from the Isa. But I'm sure George will let you drive his ute if you need to get around.'

'Okay. So, where's this home he lives in now?'

She should have known by the sympathetic smile that things were very different to what Mum had said.

'Walk down to the shops and take the second street on the left. The newsagent's on the corner. Turn left and you'll see the driveway about fifty metres down.' He nodded. 'And tell the old codger, Jack Anderson said to say hello.'

'I will, thank you.' Fallon reached into her pocket and pulled out a tattered business card. 'My mobile's on there. Give me a call when my ute's ready, or if you need me to pay for parts.'

'Ah, I know that name,' he said glancing at her card.

Fallon froze. Surely not down here?

'You're the new pilot. Heard Jon had hired a woman as well this time.'

Fallon pulled herself up straight. 'Jon? I was hired by Kent Mason. And is being a woman a problem?'

'Nuh, should it be?'

'Sorry, I cop a bit of flack sometimes.'

'Well, wait until you meet my mechanic. *She'll* tell you what the issue is with your gearbox. I'm too old to get under a car these days. I run the business, order the parts, and my daughter-in-law does the work.'

Fallon grinned. 'Good to hear it. Anyway, Jack, give me a call when she checks it out. I'll be bunking at George's house, I think. What you said about it being condemned is a bit of a worry, though.'

'It's structurally sound. It was under threat of being condemned because he's a bit of a hoarder. Always has been. I think there was a bit of finagling going on, so keep an eye out.'

'Fingaling? In what way?' This visit was getting more complicated by the minute.

'You'll see,' he said cryptically. 'Good to see family here looking out for him at last.'

'You have a visitor, George.' The aide took Fallon out to the garden where her great-uncle was sitting in the shade.

'Who are you?' The grey-stubbled cheeks were creased in deep lines.

'I'm Fallon, Sally's daughter. Your *niece*, Sally.'

'I know who Sally is. What do *you* want?'

Great start.

'I came out to see if I could give you a hand in the house to get it ready to sell, but it looks like you're all sorted. You're here already!'

A wide smile lit up his face and a memory flashed for Fallon.

'Did you show me how to pull carrots out of your veggie garden when I was a little girl?' she asked slowly.

'I did. Did I turn you into a gardener?'

Fallon sat on the bench beside him and the aide smiled before she left them alone and went back inside.

14

'I'd like to be one day when I settle. I don't have a home at the moment.'

'Why don't you have a home?' His eyes were alive with interest.

'Because I'm a pilot and I work all around Australia. I'm a contract pilot with a Western Australian company. Mustering, crop spraying, and rural firework. Keeps me busy. And when I'm not there, I like to be on a boat out to sea.'

'Ah, I get it. I'm not stupid. I read the papers.'

'Huh?' Her heart sank as she looked at him. *Did it make the papers out here too?*

'You came out here for the muster, not to see me.'

'Two birds with the one stone,' she replied.

'Have you got somewhere to bunk down?'

'Not yet. You offering?' She knew her grin was cheeky but she was enjoying the banter with Great-Uncle George.

He dug in his pocket and held up a set of keys. 'You clean my place up for me, and you can stay there. I've still gotta sell it. They let me in here on a bond, but they're waiting for their money.'

'I'm only here for three weeks so I can give you three weekends and maybe the afternoons when I knock off from the muster. Or if there's any days I don't work.' She knew there wouldn't be much chance of that unless the weather turned.

'Done deal. That's the front door key, they're the keys to the sheds, and the silver one is to my ute. I suppose you flew your plane in?'

'No, I'm a helicopter pilot. The company is sending the chopper down tomorrow.' She reached out and took the keys. 'And thank you, my ute's in the garage getting a new gearbox.'

'You take bloody good care of mine then, but like Sally said, you're cleaning up the house, so you're gonna need it.'

'So, you knew I was coming. Why didn't you tell Mum you'd moved?'

'I did, but if she knew I'd moved already, there was no need for anyone to come out. But I can't stay and chin wag. I've got a game of cards to go to. Pick any bed you want.' His wheezy laugh turned into a cough.

'Fair enough. And when I'm tidying up, is there anything I need to put aside?'

He shook his head. 'No, send it all over to your mother. She's a good stick, your mum is. She's the only one in the bloody family who rings me. Shame she couldn't come out. Would've been nice to see her before I shuffle off.'

'I'll tell her. I'm sure they'll come for a drive next time Dad's got holidays.'

With a wave of a wrinkled hand, Great-Uncle George turned his back on her and shot off after an elderly man on a walker.

'Jack Anderson said to say hello,' she called after him.

'Don't you take my chair, you old bugger,' he yelled after the man on the walker.

Fallon had left the aged care home jiggling the keys he gave her, walked down to the house and let herself in.

And now as she thought about the mess she'd stumbled into, as she leaned back on the old red ute, she ignored the compulsion to chew what was left of her nails. She'd sort something and wouldn't stress.

She scanned the sky for any sign of the helicopter. Jason was late.

A cloud of red dust lifted in the distance and as she watched, two white vehicles gradually came into view. The Landcruiser tray-back ute parked beside the hangar, and the twin cab parked at the end of the track. The driver of the tray-back rolled open the door of the hangar and jogged across to where she was leaning on Uncle George's ute.

He was a tall guy with dark hair and a wide smile, and he held his hand out to her. 'Hi, you must be Fallon. I'm Kent Mason.'

She took his hand and his grip was firm. 'Good to meet you, Kent. I was going to come over and see you at *Lara Waters* this afternoon to find out the drill. I'm just waiting for my bird to arrive.'

'You drove in?'

'Yeah, I came a little bit early, I'm helping clean out my uncle's house in town. I'm waiting for my bird now.'

He nodded as he looked at the red vintage ute.

'Ah, Mason. I didn't twig. You're related to George?'

'That's right.'

Sympathy crossed his face. 'If you need a hand . . .'

Fallon chuckled. 'I'm right for the time being, but I'll keep that in mind. So, okay to call over to see you this afternoon?'

Kent shook his head. 'We've had some changes. Don't worry, your contract's still good. Braden and I are flying to North Queensland now, but Braden's new manager at *Kilcoy Station,* Jon Ingram, is in charge of the muster. I was going to call you tomorrow. I didn't think you'd be here yet. There's a meeting out at the station tomorrow afternoon. Braden and I will be back late tonight. Come out and meet everyone tomorrow. I'll introduce you to Braden now.'

Jon Ingram? If Fallon had known he was in charge, she would have declined the contract. She'd never met him, but she'd heard his reputation around the traps.

Didn't like women on his team, was pedantic, and was difficult to talk to.

As they walked over towards the vehicle, three small boys climbed out of the twin cab ute. Their mother walked around the front of the twin cab and took the smallest boy's hand.

The other guy came out of the hangar and put his arms around the woman. Their voices carried across as she followed Kent.

'I'll see you tonight, love.'

'I'm looking forward to meeting Sophie. I hope she's okay.'

'She will be, when we get her home.'

Kent stepped forward. 'Braden, Callie, this is Fallon. Fallon, Braden owns *Kilcoy Station.*'

'Good to have you onboard, Fallon.' Again, her hand was taken in a firm grip, by Braden this time, and the woman with the curly dark hair smiled at her.

'Welcome, Fallon. Good to meet you,' Callie said. Her smile was kind and Fallon felt untidy and weather-beaten beside her. She brushed her hands down her jeans. Uncle George's ute was as dusty as the house, and that was saying something.

Kent looked at his watch. 'Braden, we'd better get going. We've got a big day ahead.'

'Yes, the sooner we get there, the happier I'll be.' Braden leaned over and kissed Callie again before he ruffled the little boy's hair. 'You be a good boy for Callie today, won't you, Petie?'

'I will.'

'Rory, Nigel, we're going now. Come and give me a hug.'

In a flurry of dust and flailing limbs, the two older boys ran over, hugged their father, and took off to the pile of dirt beside the hangar where they'd already made a track for a couple of toy cars.

'Leave the helicopter on the left-hand side of the apron. How's your pilot getting back to base?' Kent asked.

'He's getting picked up in town in a company vehicle. They're heading to Brisbane for a meeting. It saved me a big drive.'

'Okay. We'll catch up at the meeting tomorrow. You'll be flying tandem with me. My chopper's out at my place. Oh, I almost forgot. Jon asked me to text you his number, but I can give you his card. Maybe give him a call and let him know you're here?'

'Sure. I'll call him after I drop Jason off in town.' She slid the card into her jeans pocket. Might as well get it over with and suss the new boss out in person.

Fallon stood beside Callie and Braden as Kent taxied the small Cessna out of the hangar. When it was on the tarmac, Braden jumped in and with a final wave, the plane was soon at the end of the runway lifting off into the air.

'Are you from around here, Fallon?' Callie let go of the little boy's hand and he ran across to the other two.

'No. I'm only here for the contract. I'm based in the Top End, but I was originally from Brisbane.'

'Me too. I can't get over how busy it is out here. I imagined country life would be quiet.'

'You and Braden and the boys haven't been here long?'

Callie's face flushed a deep pink. 'I haven't been here long. Just a few weeks. I came out to look after the boys.'

'But you knew them before?'

She shook her head, and her cheeks stayed pink. 'No. Braden and I—God, it's complicated, sort of. Ours is a new relationship. It just happened. Don't get me wrong. I haven't stepped in as a—'

Fallon put her tanned hand on Callie's arm. 'Hey, you don't have to justify yourself to me. If you guys have hit it off, and you're happy, that's great.'

'Thank you. I feel a bit self-conscious.'

'No need to. Life's taught me not to worry about what anyone thinks.'

'You said you were going into town to drop someone off?'

'Yes.' Fallon pulled out her phone and checked the time. 'He's a bit late. His lift will be waiting for him.' As she spoke, the familiar throb of a helicopter came from the north. 'Ah, here he is now.'

'I'm taking the boys into town for a milkshake. It'd be nice to have some grown-up company. Fancy a coffee?'

Fallon smiled. 'Sounds good to me.'

Chapter 2

Augathella
Callie

Callie and Fallon sat in the park with coffee and cake as the boys played and climbed up the pole that held the giant Meat Ant sculpture.

They'd hit it off, and when they'd discovered they were the same age and had grown up in Brisbane only a suburb apart, they felt like old friends. When the boys got bored and they finished their coffees, Fallon suggested that they go back to the house, so Callie could see for herself she wasn't exaggerating.

'Oh my goodness!' Callie knew her eyes were like saucers as Fallon led her down the hallway of her uncle's house The boys were in the backyard playing on a tyre swing hanging from a tree after Fallon insisted on checking it for spiders before the boys took turns swinging. Callie followed Fallon through the front door and her eyes widened.

'Oh heck, I see what you mean,' she said.

'Mum told me to mow and tidy up the yard to make it look presentable.' She couldn't help the chuckle. 'I wonder which shed the mower's in.'

They walked down the hall through piles of junk until they reached the back door and Fallon gestured across the untidy grass where the boys were playing.

'So yeah, Uncle George has sold off a couple of thousand acres, but . . .' She stood with her hands on her slim hips. Even with her dusty jeans and battered Akubra, Callie thought what an elegant woman she was. She'd have never picked her for an outback pilot.

'But?' Callie prompted.

'Well, he sold the biggest section, but there are still ten acres full of junk. I think outside is worse than the house, and I haven't even looked in the sheds.'

'Worse than the house?' Callie looked around. 'It's a fire hazard.'

'Not to mention vermin.'

Callie shivered and looked down half-expecting to see a rat's nest at her feet.

Fallon rolled her eyes. 'I don't think Mum had any idea how bad he'd let it get. He's lived here since he was born. Never married, no family, but look at what he's collected.' She pointed to an old fashioned cane pram in the hallway behind them. 'Uncle George never had kids so I'm guessing that's the cane pram *he* slept in ninety years ago.'

'That's incredible.' Callie walked over and looked at the dust-covered pram. 'It's an antique, you know. It's probably valuable. You'll never know what's in the house until every room and every cupboard is checked. Thoroughly. There could be some valuable items in here.'

'And lots of junk. But, you're right. I think I need to have a sort out, and then Mum needs to send an appraiser out.' Fallon pulled a face. 'It's kind of sad though. This was his life and he had no one to share it with. Now he's gone into aged care and no one cares about what he's left behind.'

Callie stared at Fallon as a strange, sad expression crossed her new friend's face. 'You do. And your mum does. He has family who cares.'

Fallon nodded and after a moment seemed to shake off whatever was bothering her. 'Anyway, this isn't my first priority. I've got a contract to fulfil and three adjoining stations southwest of Augathella to fly over for the next couple of weeks.' She tapped a finger against her cheek, and Callie noticed her bitten-down nails.

'I haven't worked with Kent before. I usually fly tandem with pilots from our company. Would I be out of line if I asked you what he was like?'

'He seemed like a nice guy the couple of times I've met him. Braden and he are best mates, so that's enough for me. They grew up together. And when Braden asked him to fly to Ravenshoe, he didn't hesitate.' Callie shrugged. 'I haven't really been in town long enough to get to know many of the locals. Just some of the teachers at the school where I'm working part-time.'

'Best not to know in small towns in my experience,' Fallon said. 'I keep to myself and put my head down.'

'Let's have another coffee one day before you start working full days. Your life sounds really interesting, Fallon.'

'And you too. I'd love to hear how another Brisbane girl ended up out here.'

Callie shook her head and was pleased when the usual red cheeks stayed away. 'It's a wonder you didn't know. Most of the world does! That's a story for over a wine one night. It's a shame you have to stay in town, Fallon. There's a spare room in my accommodation.' This time her cheeks did heat as Fallon looked at her curiously. 'If you ever get sick of being in this . . . um . . . this—'

'Junkheap?' Fallon grinned. 'If it gets too bad, I might take you up on that. I thought the boys were yours, you know,' she said. 'Teaches me not to make assumptions about people, doesn't it?'

***

Fallon

26

Callie's comment came to mind as Fallon sat at a table at the Drover's Hotel later that afternoon waiting to meet with Jon Ingram. He'd sounded okay on the phone and she wondered if she'd taken too much heed of what might have been gossip from the ringer at Barkly Homestead who'd told her what a difficult boss he was.

When Jason had flown in and she'd driven him to his lift in town, she'd gone back to George's house, called Jon Ingram and organised the meeting at the pub and then worked in the house for a while.

Fallon figured she might as well start in the room she was sleeping in, and if there were any nests of anything in there, she'd get rid of them. Last night she'd slept on top of the bed and left her jeans and boots on.

This morning when she got back, she stripped the bed, and then found an old washing machine in the laundry. When she'd gone to put the grey sheets in the hot water, she took a second look, shook her head and added them to the piles of rubbish.

A foray into the cupboards lining the hall at the back of the house resulted in the discovery of half a dozen sets of new single sheets still in their wrapping. Two sheets and new pillowcases had gone into the washing machine and were now drying on the old-fashioned pole clothesline in the backyard.

She'd put two hours into that room, and when she'd discovered a vacuum cleaner—still in the box and unused—in the bottom of the same cupboard, the room had had a top-notch clean. It now held a bed, a dressing table, the walls had been wiped over, and the window sparkled. Unfortunately, the lace curtain had disintegrated in her hand when she'd taken it down to wash. The rest of the "stuff" that had filled the room, she'd dragged out to the back hallway, leaving a narrow path between the assortment of goods, so she could get to the back door.

A hot shower, clean clothes and the feeling that she had achieved something—in one room anyway—put a spring in Fallon's step as she'd walked down to the pub for her meeting.

Once she knew the work schedule, she could plan her days at the house, and hopefully make some progress.

The glass holding her lemon squash was cool against her fingers as she sat back and surveyed the pub. She could have been anywhere in outback Australia. The old chipped wooden countertop, the pool table in the corner with a dartboard on the far wall, and the pub smell. The familiar mix of sweat, spilt beer, dust, and stale cigarette smoke absorbed for years by the threadbare carpet met her when she walked in. The sour smell mixed with the lingering aroma from the loaded cattle truck that had turned to the highway at the roundabout outside as she'd walked along the wide footpath and left no doubt she was in an outback cattle town.

A beer would have gone down well after her busy afternoon, but she wanted to make a good impression on the boss.

When he arrived. She glanced down at her watch. He was already ten minutes late.

She leaned back in her chair and put her glass down as a tall man with dark hair came in the side entrance, walked across to the bar and stopped adjacent to the table she was sitting at.

A pair of piercing blue eyes in a tanned and rugged face scanned the room and settled on her for a mere second before he turned to the bar.

'Two schooners, please, mate,' he said to the barman.

Fallon turned away; for a moment she'd been sure it was Jon Ingram, but it appeared it wasn't.

Her phone buzzed in her pocket and she reached down and pulled it out and checked her messages.

I can come out the weekend after next. Cleared my schedule, so leave it free. Luv, Mum.

Fallon rolled her eyes.

Leave it free?

By then the muster would be in full swing, and she'd be working long days, weekends and all.

Didn't matter anyway. Mum could sort it out while she was at work, and she could load the ute whenever she finished.

Can you leave it free? Her phone buzzed again. **Please?**

No guarantee. Fallon quickly texted back.

Okay, I won't come.

'Shit,' she muttered sliding the phone back into her pocket. Anger simmered as she thought of all the times she'd bowed to Mum's demands. Her mother had no idea of the fact that she had a job and her own commitments. Mum could stay in Brisbane because of a bloody cake stall, but Fallon was expected to drop everything and be available to clean out the house of a man who she'd met once in her life. No wonder she didn't go home to visit much. Mum didn't put herself out, and they'd never come north to visit her. Dad had holidays every year; they could make an effort.

Why the hell she'd ever agreed to help out showed what a short memory she had. Mum was a manipulator of the first order.

'Double shit,' she muttered again.

She jumped as the chair opposite her was pulled out, and a schooner of beer appeared in front of her.

Looking up, she encountered the steady gaze of those blue eyes she'd noted and dismissed a moment ago.

The owner of them leaned over and held out a tanned hand. 'Fallon Malone, I assume?'

She nodded, took his hand and shook it, noting the calloused palms. 'Jon Ingram, I guess?'

He let go of her hand but his gaze stayed on her as he lifted the schooner and took a sip, before putting the glass down on the table.

'You're expecting someone else?' She gestured to the beer.

'It's for you. You don't look like a Chardonnay sort of girl.'

'I don't drink anything when I'm working.' She eyed the ale frothing in the schooner glass.

'You're not working now. We're just going to have a casual chat out of hours.' His voice held a husky tone, and Fallon nodded and reached for the beer.

'Thank you. That will hit the spot then I guess.'

'Are you always this edgy?'

'What?' She put the beer down and stared at him. He hadn't taken his eyes off her for a second and she felt uncomfortable, and that annoyed her.

'Your stiff shoulders, and your mannerisms. You look tense.'

Fallon forced herself to stay in the position she was in; her stance or the way she was sitting was no different to the way she always held herself. 'No. I'm not tense. I'm sitting here waiting with interest to hear about the muster, and what your expectations are.' She knew her shoulders were stiff and was surprised to see her hand clench on the table as annoyance took hold. 'Perhaps you're more used to your Chardonnay girls, Jon. Would you make that same comment to a male pilot?'

She lifted her chin as the gauntlet was thrown down. The laconic chuckle really peed her off.

'Ah, I thought that would be the case,' he said.

'The case?' The words were short and clipped.

'That's why I prefer not to have women on the job.'

'I beg your pardon? Did I hear you correctly?'

He lifted his beer and took another drink, his eyes still on her. 'You did.'

'Are you trying to deliberately piss me off with your sexist attitude?'

'I think you were already pissed off when I sat down, weren't you?'

'Whether you were right or not has nothing to do with our conversation. Tell me why you prefer not to have women on the job?'

'Because, *babe*, you all think you have to prove something, and you all have this attitude that men differentiate your ability to do the job simply because of your sex.'

'Isn't that what you were just saying?' She picked up the schooner glass, tempted to throw the beer over him, but *that* would be the sort of thing he would expect a woman to do.

He shook his head slowly from side to side. 'No. Not at all. You're the one who asked would I make the same comment to a male pilot. So you obviously have a chip on your shoulder about being looked at as a female pilot. I don't care whether you're a man or a woman. If you can fly, and follow instructions, it's irrelevant.'

Fallon drained her glass as she tried to keep calm. 'Good. I can fly.'

'And can you follow instructions?'

'If they're reasonable.'

'That's not what I asked.'

'I gave you my answer. For example, if you told me to take my chopper up, and I thought the conditions were unsafe, then, no, I wouldn't follow your instructions.'

'And why would we disagree about the conditions? You would have to give me credit for knowing my job and the conditions. I'd say I've been working with cattle since you were in nappies.'

Fallon put her glass on the table and leaned forward. 'Are you always this difficult, Mr Ingram?'

'No, but I'm always bloody thorough in choosing the right staff for the job. Lives and livelihoods depend on it.'

'I was under the impression that I had been employed by Kent Mason and that my contract was watertight. Is this a job interview, or like I said, are you just trying to piss me off?'

'Temper, temper, Fallon.' His words dripped like honey, and she stared at him wondering how such a sexy voice could come from such an obnoxious person.

At least the "babe" had taken a hike.

She went to stand. At least if she walked out of this job, she could get out of sorting Uncle George's house.

His hand shot out and grabbed her hand as her fingers gripped the edge of the table. 'We haven't finished talking yet.'

'Oh, I think we have. Let go of me. Now.'

'If you sit down and listen to me, we'll—'

'I don't particularly want to,' she said staring down at his hand on hers. Despite being callused, his fingers were long and elegant, his nails clean and clipped short, and strangely it made her dislike him even more.

His grip tightened and her temper rose.

'You've signed a contract, Fallon, and we'll sit down together and discuss your conditions of employment in a civilised fashion.' He let go of her hand and Fallon sat back down reluctantly, taking a deep breath as she held his gaze.

His eyes were intense and she found it hard not to look away. It was as though he could read her thoughts.

She'd met some hard characters in the outback, but there was something different about Jon Ingram, and she didn't know what it was.

And she didn't think she wanted to find out, she decided as a tingle headed south.

Oh, no, she wasn't going there.

Chapter 3

Fallon Malone was nothing like Jon Ingram had expected. She had a good reputation and for some reason, he'd expected her to be older, but the woman who sat so reluctantly across the table looked as though she was just out of high school. Her olive skin was flawless and huge dark brown eyes framed by long dark lashes stared back at him. For a moment he wondered if they were cosmetically enhanced, but she wore no other makeup, no lipstick and no jewellery. When she'd stood to walk out before, he'd taken note of her dress: khaki cargo shorts, an elbow-length work shirt with a white T-shirt underneath that showed off a slim build. Her straw-blonde hair was just above shoulder length and despite the no-frills, she was altogether a very feminine and attractive package. Not the sort of pilot he wanted around the ringers and stockmen who were pretty rough around the edges. Somehow he couldn't see her fitting in as one of the boys; he had a rougher than usual crew this muster. It was getting harder each year to get a team together.

'You're such a sexist pig, Jon.' He could hear Mandy's voice and he pushed it away. It had nothing to do with being sexist; it was all about making sure his team were suitable and a good fit. There was a job to be done and the dynamics of the team was his first consideration.

Okay, so he was pushing Fallon's buttons to see what sort of reaction he'd get, and he got one.

A point in her favour. She could stand up for herself. Now it was time to stop pushing and get down to business before he overstepped the mark. There was a shortage of pilots, and if she wasn't suitable, he'd have to find another one bloody quickly.

He put his glass down and leaned back in his chair. Her large brown eyes were wary as she held his gaze steadily.

'So tell me about your experience, Fallon.'

Those pretty eyes widened at the switch in his demeanour.

'My experience? I'm assuming you're talking about my flying experience?'

'I am.' He nodded and kept his eyes on her. She was a very attractive woman, and the doubts about having her in the camp wouldn't go away.

She sat straight, but the clenched hands relaxed. 'I've been flying for ten years, and I've got over six thousand hours of flying time up.'

This time it was Jon who widened his eyes as she continued.

'I got my plane license the year I left school, and my helicopter license two years after that.'

He quickly did the maths in his head; that made her close to thirty, if not past it. Close to his age. He hid a smile as he recalled his comment about her being in nappies, but it had achieved the desired effect.

'I've been working for *Wyndham Birds* for eight years now. I'm very experienced in mustering all over. Most of my work has been up in the Kimberley in Western Australia. I've done some jobs in the Gulf but this is my first time here in Southwest Queensland.'

'Okay, so we'll need to go up and have a bit of a reconnoitre seeing you're not familiar with any of these properties, and the topography. The mountains to the west of Braden's spread can prove a bit difficult if the cattle head that way.'

'The cattle will head the way I send them.'

'Will they? I'm impressed. You must have some special skills, Fallon Malone. I'm yet to see that happen one hundred percent of the time.'

'I know my job,' she said simply.

Jon was impressed by her quiet confidence. Now if she could deliver what she said, he'd worry about the guys on the ground later.

'Did you fly in?'

'No, I drove in because—' She cut the words off and he was curious, but he didn't engage.

'No matter. Where's your company R22?'

'It arrived at the aerodrome this morning.'

'So how long is it here for, if you're in a vehicle?'

'As long as we need it.'

'And what's your time frame?' he asked. 'The contract is three weeks; if we go over, can you give us extra time?'

'Yes, the company always builds in a week at the end of each contract. The weather in the north can add a week or two to a muster. I'm not sure if that's the case here.'

'Good,' he said briskly. 'I'll meet you at the aerodrome in the morning.'

Her delicate eyebrows rose. 'So I am still employed by you?'

'And why would you think you weren't?'

She stared at him, her gaze cold and the fingers he'd noticed clenched on the table earlier clenched again.

'I just assumed you'd changed your mind.'

'I'm happy with what I've heard here but I want to see you fly tomorrow. This muster is huge and the way things have been out here lately, our three property owners need a damn good job done and a fast job.'

'I don't call three weeks a fast job.'

'No, but it's a big job and we'll be doing it properly. Okay?' He pushed his glass away and stood. 'I'll meet you at the airfield at 6.30 a.m.'

He grinned at the muttered, 'Aye, aye, captain,' behind him as he walked away.

Chapter 4

Fallon ordered a takeaway burger and chips from the pub before she headed back to George's house. She planned to make a start on the kitchen having been instructed to not be late, so she'd have an early night.

She'd go out to the aerodrome early. It would be light enough by then to do the safety checks, and be ready to go when the "boss" arrived. It really irked her that she had to prove herself; her references were top notch, she was the pilot in most demand up north, and the company had recently paid her a great bonus for her work last year. She'd used it to increase her life and medical insurance cover; when she'd told Dad what she was paying for insurance, he'd been stunned.

'Don't you tell your mother that. She has no idea how dangerous your job is.'

'I'm careful, Dad. But if anything happened, I've still got a mortgage to worry about. And it never hurts to have income protection insurance.'

'I know you're careful, but I still worry.'

And this—*this cowboy*—wanted to see her in action before he'd commit. She'd show him action. With a bit of luck, he'd get airsick.

And what a cowboy; with his slicked-back dark hair, neatly pressed clothes, and manicured fingernails, he looked more like a cowboy from the movies than one of the rugged cattlemen she was used to working with.

But she thought with a shrug as she waited for her food order, he seemed to be a good operator, apart from his attitude.

A strange guy. The ringer she'd spoken to at Barkly Homestead had picked him right.

'Number six takeaway,' the woman behind the pub bistro counter called and Fallon walked over to collect her order.

'Here you go, lovey,' the woman said, handing over the white bag. She looked at Fallon with a smile. 'New in town?'

'Working here for a few weeks.'

'You know Jon, do you?'

'No, that was a work meeting.'

'Ah. You're the lady pilot we heard about.'

Fallon nodded.

Small towns.

'A word of warning. Watch him. He's a lady-killer.'

'Oh?' Fallon tilted her head to the side. 'A lady-killer?'

'Yep, Jon boy leaves a trail of broken hearts in every town. If you're after a fling, well and good, but if you're after anything more, like a ring on the finger, run a mile when he makes the move.'

'Makes the move? I'm an employee.'

'Doesn't matter, love. You're female and you're a looker. He'll make a move; he can't help himself. Jon left a few broken hearts in town when he was working here last time.'

Fallon forced a laugh. 'I don't mix work with pleasure.'

'That's what they all say. Trust me, he won't give up.'

'Thanks for the warning,' Fallon said politely. 'And thanks for dinner.' She turned and headed out to the street.

George's ute was in the shed. Cleaning that up was another thing on her to-do list. It was too beautiful a vehicle to let go of. As she strolled down the main street from the pub, she passed a huge black RAM ute with shiny bull bars. Shaking her head, she grinned. The JI numberplates were a dead giveaway.

Just what she'd expect from such a cool dude. Or a guy who thought he was a cool dude.

Hmm. A lady-killer, hey? He was a good-looking man, but she was not one bit attracted. Okay, so he was a looker, but his personality? Nuh. If she chose to sleep with anyone, she was picky, and his attitude had put her right off from the outset.

43

She crossed the road and turned the corner and put her head down as she spotted the owner of the flash ute himself standing outside the pub.

A pretty young woman leaned against the wall, smiling up at him, and Jon leaned forward one arm outstretched and his palm against the wall beside her head. As Fallon hurried past, his words reached her.

'It's good to see you, Soph. And don't worry, he's not worth it. I'll look out for you.'

Typical, she thought. Obviously stepping into someone else's territory. She kept walking without a backward glance.

Fallon was in a deep sleep dreaming of a roller-coaster ride in her bird with Jon Ingram white-faced beside her, begging her to land.

'Not until you leave that poor, young girl alone,' she said as she dived the machine nose down.

She reached for the controls as an alarm rang stridently in the cockpit. Fallon looked around trying to see where it was coming from but the sound was overpowering. She'd never heard an alarm like that before. She flicked switch after switch on and off, but the alarm still blared. She looked at Jon's white face and, even though she wondered what was happening to her helicopter, she felt satisfaction at the fear in his eyes.

God, I'm a bitch, she thought in her dream. But he deserved it.

The alarm kept ringing and ringing, and gradually she surfaced out of her deep sleep.

Bloody hell, it was a telephone. She hadn't even known there was one in the house.

Fallon jumped out of bed, stubbing her toe on the cast-iron base of the bed.

'Shit, shit, shit.' She grabbed her foot, certain she'd broken something. Limping out of her room, she followed the sound of the ringing down the hall and into the dining room, past piles of newspapers and cardboard boxes full of tarnished trophies. She hadn't noticed them before and wondered what he had trophies for.

Making her way through the mess in the passageway that had been left between the piles of junk, she spotted the phone over on an old sideboard against the far wall. She grabbed the receiver and picked it up; the phone was a 1970s vintage with the circular dial pad, but it obviously still worked. She picked it up from the cradle, her eyes roaming over the beautiful piece of furniture she hadn't noticed behind the piles of junk. The sideboard was a genuine antique and with a good dust and polish, it would be beautiful.

'Hello,' she said quickly.

'Hello. Is that George's niece?' an unfamiliar woman's voice asked.

'Yes, it's Fallon Malone here. I'm George's great-niece. Who is calling, please?

'Sorry to ring you so late, love. It's Mary from the Quiet Whispers Nursing Home.'

Fallon glanced down at her watch she'd worn to bed because she had the alarm set for four-thirty. She squinted. It was just past midnight. Dread pooled in her stomach as she realised the only reason the home would be ringing would be to tell her there was a problem with George. 'What's wrong? Is he . . . is he . . . has he. . .?'

'No, George is fine,' the woman said. 'Well, he's not exactly fine. He's very distressed and we've tried to calm him as best we could but he won't settle unless you come to see him.'

'What? Now? It's the middle of the night,' Fallon replied.

'I know.' The words were followed by a sigh. 'I wouldn't have called if there'd been any other solution. He's usually one of our best-behaved residents. He's got a bee in his bonnet about you being in the house, and that you've taken off and stolen his ute and something from his bedroom.'

'What! He gave me the keys to his ute! Stolen exactly what from his bedroom?' Fallon said

46

nursing her still throbbing foot. The worst she could be accused of was throwing out a pair of ancient mildewed sheets. 'I haven't even been in there. In fact, I don't even know which is his bedroom in this house. Have you been here? Do you know what I'm saying? Have you seen this house?' Her voice was shrill as she woke fully.

'Yes, dear, I know. I was part of the team that did his aged care assessment. The state of the house was one of the reasons he was fast-tracked. It was obvious he was incapable of caring for himself.'

Fallon shook her head and rubbed her eyes with the back of her spare hand. When did this become her problem? Mum could get the next bus out here, pronto. Before she could speak, the aide continued.

'He's got himself in a real state. Is there any chance you could just slip on some clothes and pop over? I know you're not far away from us. Come down and bring what George wants to see and just reassure him that you're still here and that you haven't got any bad intentions. Please?'

Fallon sighed and ran a hand over her hair. 'What exactly does he want and where do I find it?' she said more patiently than she felt.

'Apparently in his bedroom, under the end of the bed, there's a box with a pink lid and inside is all his precious stuff.'

'Stuff?'

'Look, it's probably not precious in terms of value. Just some memento he's attached to. He wants to be reassured that it's still there. We tried to get him to bring some possessions when he came to us, but the ambulance brought him here one night when he had a turn. All he had was the PJs he was wearing. We've asked several times if he wants one of us to go to the house and get some of his things. We find that usually settles our residents, but he refused point-blank. So with his aged care package, he had new clothes and toiletries purchased for him. He's never seemed interested in the house, but something on TV tonight set him off after dinner. He started yelling about this dreadful niece who was in his house. To clean him out of his fortune, he said.'

'Oh, for God's sake,' Fallon said. 'And you want me to come and see him while he's abusing me?'

'Yes please.' The voice was timid.

'All right. I'll come down now. I'll leave this box at—if I find it—at reception.'

'Um, no he wants to see you too. Just to be reassured that you're still here. I'm so sorry, Fallon, but he's keeping most of the floor awake with his yelling and his abuse.'

'What brought it on? He was fine when I saw him yesterday.'

'It's dementia. We've had to restrain him tonight. It's very sad but there's just no stopping him. You'll be okay. We've given him a little bit of a sedative but he's still carrying on, so if you can just grab that box and wander down, it'll only take fifteen minutes or so and then you can go home and get tucked up into bed again. I'm really sorry.'

'I'm on my way.' Fallon knew her voice wasn't over-friendly, but she was awake now. She might as well help them out. She walked along the hall and opened each door as she went. There were five other bedrooms and each room was filled with piles of junk, boxes and old newspapers just like the dining room.

Finally, she reached the one at the far end that seemed to have a bit more space in it.

'Gah.' She knew she was in the right room by the glass of clear liquid with a pair of false teeth on the side table next to the bed.

Poor guy. He didn't even have his teeth with him, she thought. She hadn't noticed his lack of teeth yesterday.

Dropping to her knees at the side of the bed released a cloud of dust. Leaning over, she lifted the faded chenille bedspread, unsure of what she would see under there. A pair of golden eyes looked back from the depths and Fallon jumped to her feet with a scream.

'Holy shit, what's that?' she yelled to an empty house.

A plaintive meow reassured her it wasn't a rat about to launch itself at her.

'Here, puss, puss, puss,' she called softly.

A thin black cat with a gleaming coat sidled out from under the bed and rubbed itself against her bare feet with another soft meow. Fallon dropped to her knees again and looked underneath the bed. Sure enough, there was a box with a pink lid. She slid it out. Although she was curious about his life, she had no intention of looking inside. She'd deposit it at the aged care home, and let Uncle George see she hadn't absconded with his worldly goods. She was learning enough about him from the contents of the house.

As she walked down the hall back to her clean room the cat followed her.

'How long have you been under there, puss?' All the doors and windows were locked, so the cat had obviously been locked inside unless it had a secret exit. She wrinkled her nose, wondering where the cat had been doing its business. Maybe that was part of the gross smell in the house. Then again, maybe not. Quickly pulling her cargo pants and work shirt over her PJs, she slipped into a pair of boots, put the box under one arm and opened the front door. The cat shot out obviously in dire need or looking for food.

'I'll feed you when I get back,' she said as she marched down the road to the aged care home.

Chapter 5

The next morning

Jon Ingram waited in his car as the sun cleared the flat horizon, golden rays fanning the dawn sky. He'd suspected Fallon would get to the aerodrome early to impress him, so he'd arrived about five-forty-five a.m. Now as he looked at his watch for the fifteenth time in as many minutes and there was still no sign of her, he was unimpressed. She was almost fifteen minutes late.

He'd read her wrong. He thought she'd be here at sparrow fart. But she was obviously playing games by being deliberately late. He'd give her another fifteen and she was out. Contract or not, he wouldn't put up with someone unreliable.

Fourteen minutes later, at one minute to seven, when he'd been sitting there for an hour and a half, Jon sat up straight as a classic car tore along the road next to the aerodrome.

Low to the ground, the red, vintage F100 ute was in perfect condition, albeit a little dusty. It veered into the aerodrome, almost on two wheels—whoever was driving it was skilled—and kicked up dust as it approached the hangar where the helicopter was sitting. He got out of his RAM, car-envy surging through him as the throaty roar of a souped-up 351 cubic inch V8 broke the early morning silence. Whoever owned it, he'd make them an offer they couldn't refuse.

He *had* to have it.

His eyes widened with surprise when Fallon almost fell out of the driver's seat and ran barefooted over to the chopper. Long bare legs ending at a minuscule pair of pink—*pink*—shorts flashed past him as she ran bare-footed towards the machine. She glanced at him and didn't speak as she leaned against the side of the machine and pulled on the pair of work boots she carried. As he walked over he saw the look of horror that crossed her face as she looked down at the pink shorts.

As he got closer, he realised they weren't shorts, but looked like PJs.

Rather than balling her out as he'd intended over the past half hour, he couldn't help the belly laugh that rose from his gut.

'Love the look, Fallon. I've never had a pilot take me up in their PJs before. Goes nicely with the work boots.'

'Don't. Just don't,' she said. 'I apologise for my appearance, and I apologise for my lateness, so just leave it there, okay?' She stood straight and he couldn't help his eyes dropping to that gorgeous pair of legs that seemed to go forever. His lips twitched as he saw the cute little teddy bears on her pink PJ shorts.

'Okay. I will. Next time, just set an alarm.'

'I did.'

'Well, next time, wake up.'

If looks could kill, he would have sizzled on the spot.

'I just have to do the safety check and probably top up with fuel.'

'How about I go to the bakery and get us both a coffee while you do that?' He turned to the car. 'Love your wheels. 1962? Can I take it for a spin into the bakery?'

She hesitated and looked at him.

He glanced at the ute and grinned at her. 'Coffee *and* Danish pastries?'

'All right. Don't prang it. It's not mine.'

'Way to go.' He grinned at her. 'How long do you need?'

'It all depends. How much of a hurry are you in? What time do we have to be back?'

'We've got all morning. Or I have. We're meeting with the team at two this afternoon out at Braden's station.'

'In that case, can we delay our departure a little? I'll let you drive the ute and get the coffee if you drop me off back in town and I can get dressed properly.' Her face was as pink as her PJ pants.

With a chuckle, he nodded. 'Jump in and tell me where to go.' He shot a sideways look at her. 'Literally, that is. Not what you're thinking. Where you're staying.'

Fallon opened the passenger door and climbed up, and Jon walked around to the driver's side. He smoothed his hand over the beautiful paintwork before he got in.

'What a bloody beauty,' he said.

'Yeah, my ute's in dock. Needs a new gearbox, so I've been driving this one.'

He started the engine and closed his eyes as the V8 burbled. 'Who owns it?'

There was no reply and he looked over at her. 'Does it matter?'

'Yep. I want to buy it.'

'Ha, good luck with that. If you do, it's got nothing to do with me. After the night I've had, I'm not going there.'

'So who owns it?'

'My great-uncle.'

He nodded. 'Okay, so where am I taking you?'

'Go past the pub where we met yesterday, and then take the second left. The last house in the street on the edge of town.'

Jon did as he was instructed, checked the bakery was open as he drove past, and then took the second left. It was a long street and the last house was set back from the road, surrounded by half a dozen sheds.

'A farm once?'

'Apparently ten thousand acres. Still on ten acres now.' Her voice held something that showed she was unhappy about that.

'Okay, I'll drop you off and go and grab us some breakfast. Do you need the car keys or is there someone to let you in?'

'No, thank you. I put the front door key under the mat.'

'Is that safe?'

'In this town? I think so. I was walking through town at two a.m. and didn't see a soul. And no, I hadn't been out having a good time.'

'You can tell me that story later. I'll be back in ten or so. What sort of coffee?' Fallon Malone was turning into an interesting person.

'Cappuccino, please. Double shot. Thank you.' It must have been hard, but she lifted her head and looked at him once she was out of the car. 'I mean it. Thank you, and I promise I won't let you down again.'

'Babe.' He couldn't help himself and then felt mean when she visibly cringed. 'You're forgiven.

Letting me drive this gorgeous beast has put me in your debt. Not to mention the PJs.'

'Good.' Finally a smile tilted her pretty lips, and Jon found it hard to look away as attraction tugged.

'I'll go and get some work clothes on,' she said as he pushed the unwanted attraction away.

He didn't get involved with anyone he worked with, contrary to his reputation. He'd knocked back a couple of offers of a night out—or in—and the gossip mill had started.

'If you must. I didn't see a problem with your teddy bear PJs,' he teased.

She pulled a face at him and slammed the door before she hurried along the path, bending down and scooping up a black cat when she reached the front porch.

Jon did the gentlemanly thing and looked away because it was obvious she was wearing nothing beneath the teddy bear pyjama pants.

Chapter 6

Waves of embarrassment rolled over Fallon as she stood under the shower. Jon had said ten minutes until he came back and she headed straight to the bathroom and turned the tap to be greeted with lukewarm water. There was some maintenance needed on the house, but whoever bought it could deal with that. You pretty much had to run around under the showerhead to get wet in both the showers in George's house.

As soon as her great-uncle had seen her last night and she'd handed over the pink-lidded box, he'd smiled.

Poor George.

'Sally! Thank you,' he'd said, mistaking her for Mum. 'That daughter of yours didn't take them. Thank heavens!' He hugged the box to his chest and a single tear ran down his face. 'I don't want to lose my Josie's letters. I don't care if that girl's stolen my ute.'

'No, Uncle George. Everything is in your house. And the ute is in the shed,' Fallon said quietly as she exchanged a sad smile with the aide, and wondered who Josie was. When she'd come here to see him earlier, he'd been lucid. It was sad to see a huge strapping man like Great-Uncle George with his mind deteriorating.

'What's your cat's name?' she asked softly as he stared at her.

'Sooty. You know that, Sally, I've always had a Sooty,' he said with a nod. 'She won't eat fish. Just chicken. Ask Reg at the butcher. He'll get the right ones for you, all chopped up and then put the chicken meat through the cast-iron mincer on the edge of the kitchen bench.'

'I will,' Fallon promised. And made a mental note she'd also need to find a new home for Sooty before she headed north again.

Mary walked her to the door. 'I'm sorry I had to call you. That's the first bad episode he's had. He's a lovely old guy and usually pretty good. He had a fall at the dinner table last night, and we're worried he's had a TIA. He was a bit confused for a while and came good. Then he had his big panic when he woke up a couple of hours ago. The doctor will see him in the morning.'

'TIA?' Fallon queried.

'A little brain bleed. It can be the precursor of a stroke.'

Fallon had walked slowly back to the house and lay there awake for a long time before she'd drifted into a deep sleep.

And then she damn well slept through her watch alarm and woke up at 6.45. In a panic, she'd grabbed her shirt and boots and George's car keys, and it wasn't until she was standing by the bird that she'd looked down and mortification flooded through her when she realised she was still wearing her pyjama pants. It had been the night *before* she'd slept in her jeans, *not* last night.

In her half-asleep mad panic, she hadn't even looked down as she'd grabbed her boots and run out to the shed. As she'd driven through the quiet town, her attention had been totally on the road, as she broke every speed limit, and she hadn't even noticed her bare legs.

Her face burned now as she quickly dried herself. She would never live that down, and she really hoped Jon would keep that to himself. Not the sort of story to be shared around a muster campfire.

She ran a comb through her wet hair, pulled on her cargos, a clean black T-shirt and work shirt, and then put the key back under the mat. The cat—Sooty—had disappeared in the house somewhere. She'd pick up some cat food—the chicken from Reg the butcher—and sort her out when they got back.

Seven minutes after Jon dropped her off she was waiting on the grass outside the rusted front gate when he pulled up.

'I'm impressed,' he said with a smile as she opened the door and then lifted the cardboard holder with two coffees in it.

'With?' Fallon forced confidence and sass into her voice and body language.

'Your speed. And you've had a shower too. Most impressive.'

'I'll be even more on the ball when I have a coffee. Which one's mine?'

'Both the same.'

'Thank you.'

'Just as well you had to go home. I wouldn't fancy going up in the air with you if you weren't on the ball.'

'Don't worry. I would have been. The coffee just gives me more energy. I wouldn't fly if I didn't feel up to it.'

She sipped her coffee and looked through the window as they passed the Big Meat Ant on the pole, crossed the wide sandy river bed of the almost-dry river, and then headed up the Old Tambo Road towards the aerodrome.

Jon turned the ute along the red dirt road into the aerodrome, came to a slow stop and cut the engine. His smile was wide. Fallon smiled back as he patted the steering wheel with a reverence that she understood.

'That's how she deserves to be driven,' he said.

'She's a beauty, isn't she?' she said. 'I'll be sorry to leave her here.'

'Absolutely original condition. Except I think the motor's been hotted up.'

Fallon shrugged. 'Don't know her history.' Maybe she'd talk to Mum and see what would be involved with her buying it. She knew Mum and Dad were the executors of Uncle George's will.

She frowned. Was that what Mum had been hinting at about the house? Gawd, that was the last thing she wanted to be lumbered with; inheriting that house would be a nightmare. Hopefully, Uncle George had a few years in him yet, although that TIA thing sounded a bit of a worry.

'Any chance of it being for sale?'

'What, the house?'

Jon shook his head. 'Are you sure you're awake? Is there any chance of this gorgeous vehicle being for sale?'

'Sorry. I was thinking about the house. If the ute's for sale, I'll be first in line,' she said. Fallon tossed him a glance, hoping that answer didn't put him into a bad mood again; she was still wary.

'Shame. I'd be happy to take it if you change your mind.' He was still smiling. Certainly a different mood to the one he'd been in at the pub yesterday. Maybe he'd got lucky, last night. He was in a damn fine mood this morning.

'I'll note that.'

'Good.' He reached between the seats and retrieved a bakery brown paper bag. 'I bought two sorts of Danish because I didn't pick you as an apple girl.'

'Is that the same failing as a Chardonnay girl?' Fallon couldn't help asking. If he could be pleasant so could she.

He grinned back. 'I thought the apricot one was a bit sweeter.'

'So I needed sweetening up, did I?' Fallon took the bag he passed over.

'No comment.' His grin widened and the tanned skin around his eyes crinkled.

'You weren't Mr Personality yourself at the pub yesterday.'

'I'm the boss.'

'Yeah and I'm the employee. Two-way respect is what I'm used to getting.' She looked across at him as he sipped his coffee. 'Aren't you eating?'

He reached over and she froze as his thumb wiped the side of her mouth. An exquisite tingle fired in her nerve endings, and they weren't the nerves around her mouth.

'You're covered in icing sugar. And no, I'll leave my *apple* Danish in the car until we come down.'

Fallon nodded slowly as understanding dawned. She ignored the increased heartbeat; that was the sugary Danish causing it to race. Nothing else. 'You don't get airsick, do you?'

'Depends on how good the pilot is.'

'Oh, I'm good,' she said. 'Don't you worry about that. But I'll be gentle with you.'

'Thank you. I like a woman who's gentle.' Their eyes met and held and she was the first to look away.

'Anyway, that's good to hear in regard to your *flying*, but I'll still leave breakfast until we get back.' He drained his coffee cup and she looked at him curiously, wondering if he really did get airsick.

He'd been nice this morning, so maybe she would give him an easy ride, and not the roller coaster one she'd dreamed about last night. That must have been her self-protective subconscious kicking in.

'Okay.' Fallon picked up her coffee and drained the last of it. 'Thanks for breakfast and again, I'm sorry I was late.'

'Come on, let's get this show on the road. We've got quite a bit of ground to cover.'

'Which direction are we heading?' Fallon looked across at the windsock at the side of the aerodrome, but it barely moved as the occasional desultory puff of breeze drifted in. 'It's a good morning, wind wise. The sky's clear but I want to check the wind forecast on my phone. I haven't had a chance to look this morning. Just give me a minute. I'll have a look before I do the safety check.' She reached for the phone in her pocket. 'No need if the wind's not right.'

'Clear skies. Wind from the south-south-west at five kilometres. No forecast of rain or storm and no change is expected for the rest of the week. There's a high sitting smack bang above us. Can you trust me?'

'I can.' She put her phone away. 'I'm impressed you've checked.'

'I have because I need to keep a close eye on the weather too. The last thing we want over the next three weeks is rain. First week is looking good.'

'How many cattle are we bringing in?'

'1500 head on Braden's place, 2000 on Kent's and I'm still waiting to hear from Craig Wilson. He'll be at the meeting at *Kilcoy Station* this afternoon.'

'There'll be a few trucks in.'

'Yep, we use a local company.'

'Do they export from Darwin?'

'No, Port Alma near Rocky. A third of the distance. Only seven hundred ks.'

'Much better.' She nodded. 'And which direction are we going in this morning?'

'South-south-west,' he said as he went to pass her the ute keys and open the driver's door. 'Or do I need them to lock from the driver's side?'

'Yes. I think so.'

Jon took the keys back and once she'd put her window up, climbed out and closed the door, he used the key to lock the driver's door.

Fallon tested her door, and it was locked. Last thing she wanted after George's rant was to have the vintage ute stolen. She'd take more care locking the shed at night from now on too.

They walked over to the helicopter together.

'The three properties cover about a hundred kilometres to the west and another seventy-five to the south. We'll do the boundary run first and I'll show you where the stockyards and muster camps are. We'll be mustering towards three stockyards. One for each property on their shared boundaries.'

'Okay.'

'Have you met Kent yet or did he call you?'

'I met both Braden and Kent yesterday morning when I was out here waiting for the chopper to come in. They were flying north apparently. I assume they're back. I had coffee with Callie afterwards. She was friendly.'

'Yes, they're back. They went to pick up Braden's sister. That was Sophie I was talking to when you passed us outside the pub last night. And yeah, Callie's the best thing that could have happened to Braden,' he said, but didn't elaborate.

'Good.' She nodded, not quite sure if she should respond. She was here to work. Not to get to know everyone's issues, even though she and Callie had clicked instantly.

'Hey, you don't know anyone looking for a job out here, do you?'

'What sort of job?'

'Braden's looking for a housekeeper and a governess. It's hard to get staff out here and keep them.'

'I'll keep an ear out, but I don't really meet many people on the properties. Just the muster camps. But sometimes you hear stuff.'

'No friends looking for a job?'

Fallon shook her head. 'I don't socialise much. I'm usually too busy.'

He looked at her curiously but agreed. 'Yeah, I know what that feels like.'

Fallon walked around the machine and carried out the safety checks. Jason had filled the tank for her before he'd left so it was all good. She walked around the bird, lifted the cowl and checked the fuel lines.

***

Jon stood back waiting while Fallon did the safety check. He swallowed back the nausea that threatened and made sure his stance was confident and his expression bland. He held the greatest admiration for the muster pilots, but she didn't need to know that yet. Fallon also didn't need to know how much he hated being up in the air. Give him a horse any day.

So far he was impressed with how she was handling her job. Economy of movement and a keen eye as she looked around the chopper. Her concern with the weather, plus her sense of humour, combined into a bit of a mystery package. Shame she was an employee; he would have enjoyed getting to know her better and spending some time with her.

Yesterday in the pub he knew he'd pushed her buttons, and his first impression hadn't been favourable, but when Fallon had dropped the sass and shown some vulnerability this morning, his opinion had changed. He'd actually felt sorry for her. He'd love to know what she was doing wandering around town at two o'clock this morning, but he guessed he'd never know.

And it's none of your business. As long as it didn't impact her ability to do her work.

But even yesterday in the pub he'd sensed something underneath and he wanted to get to the bottom of it, so he'd taken the sexist line to get a reaction. Maybe it had been the wrong thing to do, but, God, women, he thought, why can't they just be like blokes? With blokes, what you see is what you get.

But to be fair, Jock Evans, Sophie Cartwright's ex, had pulled the wool over everyone's eyes.

After he'd caught up with Sophie briefly at the pub last night, he'd had a quick beer with Braden and Kent. They'd driven into town because Sophie had wanted to stay with a friend and not go out to the property. When he'd been talking to her, Fallon had scurried past with her head down, all adding to today's perception that she was a private person who kept to herself.

Sophie was the opposite. He'd had to excuse himself because she'd wanted his sympathy, and wanted to tell him all about what had happened between her and Jock. Braden had told him enough for him to know that Sophie was pretty fragile, so he'd untangled himself gently from the conversation, with a promise to catch up later. They'd been good mates when he'd worked out at *Kilcoy Station* before, and Jock had just come on the scene. A good bloke, sociable, and a hard worker. He'd muscled in and broken up Kent and

Sophie, that was the one negative in Jon's book. But Sophie was grown up, and it was for her to choose.

But she'd chosen the wrong man, well and truly. Braden didn't go into detail, but it sounded as though she'd been through a pretty hard time.

'Okay, Mr Boss. A bit late, but looks like we're ready to go. Climb in.'

Jon pushed Sophie to the back of his mind. At least he'd stopped thinking about flying for a while. 'Not *too* late.'

Fallon obviously had a reason for being late, and he respected that circumstances could change plans. He was reassured now; it wasn't disorganisation. She'd obviously had some sort of drama through the night. He stifled a grin. As long as everything was fine, it didn't matter. Fallon turning up in cute, brief pyjama pants had been a bonus.

Her demeanour this morning had been pleasant and efficient and he'd seen a glimmer of that sense of humour a couple of times.

Jon strapped himself in and took the headset she passed over, chastising himself mentally. It didn't matter whether he liked her or not. She was an employee. He needed to get his head back on the muster and away from the attractive woman who was about to take his life in her hands. He ignored the prickle of cold sweat that formed on the back of his neck and closed his eyes as she pushed the starter.

Not that he didn't think she was a top operator. Fallon Malone had come with excellent references and a top-notch verbal reputation. He'd heard of her and her flying skills a few times when he'd been up in the Gulf but they'd never crossed paths. When *Wyndham Birds* had put her name forward for this muster, he'd accepted readily.

Jon focused on his breathing as the engine started and he knew she'd be checking the instruments and getting all the systems working.

Give me a bloody rogue horse over a manmade hunk of metal.

Pretend it's Kent, he told himself as the helicopter lifted off the ground. Jon opened his eyes and glanced across at her, but Fallon was focused on the controls and didn't look his way.

Her fingers flicked efficiently over the dials and he watched closely as she gripped the single T-bar cyclic between them. He went to lift his hands from his lap to grip the side of the seat, but he managed to resist.

'Right to go?' Her voice crackled through the headset

He nodded, and mouthed, 'Right to go' as she glanced at him.

The helicopter lifted and tilted forward as she set a bearing. Neither of them spoke until they'd gained height and headed southwest across the red dirt below.

Jon managed to get himself under control and pointed down.

'There's a couple of properties in between town and the border to Braden's place, but he's got the biggest property around so we'll hit the eastern boundary of it soon.'

Fallon's voice came through the headset again. 'The river's low.'

'Yeah, they've been in drought again over the last eighteen months. There's some water in the river, enough for them to irrigate, plus they pump from the artesian basin. There's enough water to keep the pasture up and the cattle watered. They're in good nick out here most of the time.'

'What's that down there?' She pointed ahead to a green patch that covered around a thousand hectares in front of them. 'Not often you see that much green in the outback.'

'It's an organic wheat crop. A young couple came to town a few years back just before I left the area. They decided to have a go at it. Apparently, they're going okay, lots of orders from organic stockfeed suppliers and organic chicken farmers and the like. It's their third season and they've survived.'

'Good to see some diversification,' she said.

He nodded and gestured out of his side. 'Okay, if you look across to the west you can just see a set of cattle yards. That's the northeast corner of Braden's property, and those yards are the ones where the trucks will pick his beasts up. You'll bring the cattle out furthest to another set of yards to start with, and then bring them in to here a couple of days later. The same goes for Kent and Craig's places. A temporary holding yard to start with and then they'll all come back here over seven to ten days.'

'Not good access for the cattle trucks further out where you hold them?'

He lifted his thumb. 'You got it. There's a road that comes in from the back of Charleville the cattle trucks and road trains use. If you look west you might see them on the road as we fly. A couple of the other stations are already mustering.'

Fallon nodded. 'From the air?'

'No, horseback.'

All was quiet for another ten minutes as they approached the green and red variegated landscape ahead. The ground had held the moisture of last season's rains by the look of things. As he looked at the landscape below, his focus moved from his churning stomach.

He'd conquered his nerves and looked down at the familiar channel country of south-western Queensland. It was good to be back; it was sad that he was no longer needed in Normanton, the two years had been tough. The Gulf was different, but he was grateful his employer there had been so understanding He'd missed this landscape, he felt at home here, and Jon had been pleased when he'd heard Braden was looking for a manager. When he'd called, there'd been no hesitation on either side, and he figured he'd stay as long as Braden needed him this time. He had no commitments anymore.

'It's different to the north,' Fallon said. 'Not as much vegetation and no trees and only low scrub. That's fabulous for us.'

'Fabulous? How? For who?' He frowned.

'"Dead man's zone" we call it. Flying low and flying slow when mustering, you don't have time to react if a tree suddenly appears in front of you. And if there are trees, that's where the cattle like to get.' Her voice was tight and he noticed her hand tensed.

'I honestly don't know how you do it. I apologise for being flippant yesterday. It's not a career for the faint-hearted. I have the utmost respect for what you do.'

'And I respect you guys on horseback. I'm terrified of the bloody things.'

Before he could reply, the chopper shuddered as they hit an air pocket. Jon tried to remain calm and not grab hold of his seat, pleased he hadn't given in to the temptation of the Danish.

The coffee he could hold down but the last thing he wanted was to spew in front of Fallon Malone.

'Sorry,' she said. 'A bit of a bump there.' She glanced at him and frowned. 'All good?'

'I'm fine.' He tried to disguise his deep breath as he inhaled, covered his mouth and coughed. 'Just ahead to the east you'll see a shed about a kilometre away. And another set of cattle yards. That's Kent's place.'

Chapter 7

Fallon looked ahead to where Jon indicated. She was feeling sorry for him. It was obvious he wasn't a good passenger, no matter how much he tried to disguise it. He was quiet as she approached the yards.

'I see them. Will we keep going to the third station or shall we go back? I've got the lie of the land now.'

'Yeah. He lifted his arm and looked at his watch, and once again, Fallon noticed the long, fine fingers. They looked like they belonged to a concert pianist rather than a cattleman.

'And you manage Brayden's place?'

'Yeah. I've just come down from Normanton where I was looking after a couple of big spreads. I managed his property a couple of years back when he lost his wife. When he was back on deck, I had to go north, but the channel country out here is like home to me.'

'So, here to stay?'

'Looks like it. Where else have you worked?'

'Like I said yesterday, mainly in the Gulf and the East Kimberley, but it is different down here.

Should be a pretty easy muster with little vegetation.

'Strange we haven't crossed paths before. The station might cover a lot of land but it's a small cattle world. I have worked with *Wyndham Birds.*'

'Yeah.' She didn't say she had heard of him.

'If the cattle get spooked down there, nothing stops them. There's not many tracks and they scatter to the winds, so be aware of that.'

'How many ringers and stockmen on horseback?' she asked as she turned the bird back towards Augathella.

'We've got a team of about twenty and they'll rotate around the properties. Quad bikes and horseback.'

'Contract guys?'

'Yep, contract guys plus Braden and Kent and me.' He grinned. 'I'd say Sophie will be out there too, now that she's home. She's a natural on horseback. She can outride most of the guys.'

'Sounds like a good team. Always good to have the bosses out with the contract workers.'

'Will they camp out or is it close enough to the accommodation? I'm just trying to get a feel for the days and the times.'

'They'll camp out. Once the workers lived in their accommodation on the stations, but these days you tend to find they're seasonal. Plus we have a cook out there.'

'And do you find it hard to get them when you need them? The guys up north are finding it tougher each year.'

'Yes, there's a bloody shortage of good stockmen everywhere. They're all older blokes, these days. The young ones don't want to take it on.'

'Same in the north,' she said. 'Not to mention muster pilots,' she said raising her eyebrows.

'Yeah, your company assured me you had good references.'

'And I'm flying to your satisfaction.' She bit back a smile. The closer they got to the aerodrome, the more his hands relaxed.

'You are.'

'I've proved I can lift a bird off the ground and put it in the direction you told me. You still have to see ifr I can handle a cattle muster.'

Jon chuckled. 'Yep, you'll do, Miss Chardonnay.'

As they approached the aerodrome, Fallon nodded. 'I'm pleased. Thanks for showing me the land and the stations. It's given me a good idea of what to expect.'

They sat quietly once they'd landed, waiting for the rotors to slow.

Fallon made a note to refuel tomorrow. It would give her an excuse to leave Uncle George's house.

***

Jon climbed out as Fallon checked the instruments.

'Where's the meeting this afternoon?' she called as she followed him.

'It's out at Braden's.' He turned to her with a smile. Maybe you'd like to drive my work ute out and I can take the F100.'

'The RAM?'

'No, that's my good car. No one drives that.'

She chuckled. 'In that case, not a chance. I might follow you out though. I don't know this area well. I'd hate to get lost and be late twice in one day.

'Not a problem,' he said. 'Actually, I have to come back into town after the meeting. We could travel together if you like.'

Her deep belly laugh surprised him. 'You really want to drive the F100 that much?'

He grinned back at her. 'I do. And I still want to buy it.'

'I'll swap it for your RAM,' she said.

'Who owns it?' He held up his hands. 'Not that I'd go behind your back. Or swap it for my RAM.'

'My uncle. Great uncle actually. That's why I was walking through town in the early hours. And why I slept through my alarm. Don't worry. It won't happen once the muster starts. It was a one-off.'

'A problem?'

'Uncle George is in aged care, and I'm staying at his place while I'm in town. Supposed to be cleaning it up to sell, but I think it's beyond me. It needs a skip bin out the front and a few brawny blokes to carry out the entire contents. Sad, isn't it, how life ends?'

Jon lifted his head and stared past her. His mouth was set; he knew all about that. 'You collect all this stuff in your life and even though it might be important to you, no one knows when you go. And you're the only one it's important to. I feel for you. It's not a nice thing to do.'

'Poor Uncle George. I had to look for a box under a bed last night and take it to him, so the nursing home could get some peace and quiet. He thought I was my Mum.'

'Sad,' he said, his voice clipped. 'Anyway, if the ute doesn't work out for you let me know. No matter when. My mobile's on my card.'

'I will. Where's home for you,' she asked curiously.

'Wherever I'm working.'

'No base? No home?'

He shook his head. 'No.'

Fallon nodded. They had more in common than she'd realised. 'Same for me. No base. I mean I've got a room in my family home in Brisbane, but I haven't been back for a while. Plus an investment property in Cairns. I usually bunk in the accommodation on the properties, but I agreed to stay here in town and help out.'

'If you need a hand,' Jon said, wondering what the hell he was doing. The prospect of spending more time with Fallon was appealing, but he pulled himself up fast.

Don't get involved with staff.

He frowned and shook his head. 'Sorry, on second thought I'll take that back. I won't have time.'

'I don't expect anyone to help. That's not why I mentioned it.' Her voice was cold. 'I'm sorry I dumped my issues on you.'

The mood between them changed after that, the lightness and the levity disappeared.

Jon regretted it, but it was necessary. He'd let himself be too attracted and let down his guard.

'Thanks for taking me up today. You did well.' He knew by the look on her face he sounded patronising. 'I'll come to your uncle's place about two and you can follow me out.'

As much as he'd love to drive that ute again, he wouldn't be tempted. Spending more time alone with an attractive employee was not a good move.

She shrugged. 'Whatever. I'll be ready.'

Jon strode off to his ute without a backward glance. He jumped in and took off back towards town, kicking himself.

When would he ever learn?

***

Fallon lifted her hand and wiped her forehead. She looked down at it; it came away black and grimy. Once she'd got back to the house, she'd worked off her cross mood by making a start on the kitchen.

On the way, she'd called into the nursing home and checked on Uncle George, but the doctor hadn't called in yet.

'You can go and see him if you want,' the lady in reception said.

'No, I won't upset him.'

She'd left the home and gone to the butcher in town to get the chicken meat for the cat. When she'd asked for Reg, the young guy behind the counter stared at her.

'Reg? There's no Reg here.' He frowned. 'Hang on. My grandfather used to own the shop. His name was Reg.'

She'd waved a hand. 'Sorry. Someone got their wires crossed. I just want some chicken meat so I can mince it for George Mason's cat.'

'Sooty won't each chicken. Has to have veal. I'll get you some. I'll mince it for you too.'

'Thank you.' Most things about this town were good. Everyone was friendly and she'd had a warm welcome wherever she went.

Fallon fed Sooty in the kitchen, and he'd scoffed the mince and then he'd wound himself around her ankles as she opened the cupboards. Every one she peered into was full of junk. It was a daunting prospect.

Now she was head down in the kitchen and so far had found nothing worth keeping. She stood at the window over the old sink and stared out over the dead back lawn.

What was she doing here and why was she focusing on the house? Since Jon had shut down at the end of the conversation, she even wondered what she was doing out here at all.

Fallon ignored her maudlin thoughts and pulled out the Gumption and a sponge and put her cross mood into scrubbing the sink as she tried to forget how much she'd liked Jon Ingram for a short while.

After a shower and a change of clothes, she backed the F100 out of the locked shed and was waiting outside the house on the road when Jon pulled up in a dust-covered work ute

He pulled up on her driver's-side, lowered the passenger window and called out, 'You right to go?'

The friendly expression was still missing; the man from the pub yesterday was back. Fallon nodded and gave him a thumbs up and put her window up, and went to press the air conditioning button.

'Damn,' she muttered as she remembered she wasn't in her ute; she was in Uncle George's.

'Double damn,' she muttered more loudly as she followed Jon's ute down the road. She'd forgotten to check the fuel.

Nothing had gone right since she'd hit this town.

Chapter 8

Fallon glanced down at the old-fashioned semi-circular dial and was pleased to see it was three-quarters full. According to her information, the property was about forty kilometres out of town by road even though it seemed a lot less in the air this morning.

She had plenty of fuel to get out and back, so she relaxed into the drive, tagging him through town and out to the Charleville road.

It was a pleasant afternoon. The wind had come up slightly despite his forecast of no wind. She grinned at that and was cross that she was trying to get one up on him. The sky was a cloudless blue and the mountains in the distance glowed in the mid-afternoon sun.

The drive out was uneventful and after forty minutes she followed him through the gates of *Kilcoy Station.*

A dozen utes were parked along the back of a big shed down behind a large house. As she eased the ute to the end of the row, heads turned and mouths dropped. Uncle George's ute sure was a head-turner. Fallon grinned as she parked it in a sea of white work utes.

She climbed out, locked the door manually and walked over to Jon's ute as he pulled a carton of beer off the back of the tray.

'Thank you, that made it a lot easier to find the place,' she said.

'Come on, I'll introduce you to the team.' He nodded briskly.

Fallon had no choice but to follow him as they crossed the wide driveway. As she hurried to match his stride a voice called her name.

' Fallon!'

She turned around with a smile as she recognised the voice. 'Hi Callie, I'm just going to the meeting. I'll talk to you later.'

''All good. I just wanted to let you know in case Jon didn't tell you.'

'Tell me what?' Fallon raised her eyebrows.

'Braden's putting on a barbecue after the meeting. I was hoping you were going to stay.'

'I didn't know, but yes, that would be nice.'

'It won't be too late. But if you wanted to have a drink, stay over. You can have the spare room in my donga.'

Fallon waved a hand as Jon stood at the door of a big shed staring at her.

'I'll talk to you later, Callie.' She hurried towards the big corrugated iron shed.

The hum of many conversations reached her as she caught up to where Jon waited.

'So you're ready to start work finally?'

The unfairness of his comment rankled, but she ignored him. A dozen or so men in dusty work clothes stood around in a couple of groups. Most held a can of beer. She followed Jon over to the side of the shed where there were two large fridges.

'Can you open the one on the left, please?' he said with a nod at the fridge.

Fallon obliged, and after he'd slid the carton into the fridge where the shelves had been removed, he turned back and held out a stubby.

'No, thank you. I don't drink on the job.'

This time it was Jon who raised his eyebrows. He pulled the cap off his beer.

'Whatever. Find somewhere to sit.'

As she made her way over to a hay bale in the middle of the open shed close to where the men had gathered, she drew some curious looks, a few nods and a couple of hands raised in greeting.

Normally, when she was mustering up in the Gulf or Western Australia she'd know some of the ringers and stockmen, but being so far from her usual stamping ground all the faces were unfamiliar, although most of them held a welcoming smile.

'Grab a chair, grab a patch of ground or a hay bale,' Jon called over the noise as Braden and Kent walked in. 'Make yourself comfortable, guys,' he glanced at Fallon, 'and we'll let you know what's happening.'

Over the next fifteen minutes, he outlined the plan that he had given her a short version of this morning. As he spoke, Fallon was pleased that she'd done a flight over the stations with him because what he was saying made a lot more sense than it would have if she hadn't had the aerial reconnaissance of the two properties. The third one, well at least she knew where it was and what the setup was.

'So Wednesday morning,' Jon said as he wound up the talk. 'Six a.m. start. The quad bikes will head out to Braden's boundary, and those on horseback will head out to the main camp. We've got a truck arriving mid-morning with swags and supplies.' He glanced at Fallon. 'Kent and Fallon, up in the air about noon.

Fallon nodded.

Kent called out. 'Where do you want us to base ourselves with the choppers, Jon. In town at the Aerodrome where Fallon's bird is, or out at my place or here at *Kilcoy Station*?'

Jon frowned and rubbed his jaw. 'I think if you come out here to *Kilcoy* it'll be more central. Does that suit you, Fallon?'

He knew very well she had a bed in the house in town, but she'd taken notice of how long it had taken to drive out here; it just meant if the chopper was here she'd have an earlier start in the mornings.

Then she'd have to drive back into town in the afternoons if she'd planned on working on the house at night.

She lifted her hand in a casual wave. 'Not a problem.'

This was why she'd come to southwest Queensland. Uncle George's house would just have to wait. She made a mental note to call her mother later tonight. They were going to have to come and take charge.

'Okay guys, I think we're pretty organised. Bright and early Wednesday morning. Now come on over and join the barbie Braden's put on for us. I can smell the meat cooking and the beer's cold.'

Fallon wrinkled her nose as the enticing aroma of barbequing meat and onions greeted them as she walked over to the house with Kent. Jon was talking to a couple of guys, and one stared at her as she walked past with Kent. She met his gaze steadily and he looked away.

'You've settled in okay to town?' Kent asked as they walked to the house yard. 'Not working too hard in that old place of George's?'

ANNIE SEATON

Fallon chuckled. 'I could work there every day for a year, I think, and I wouldn't get anywhere near the bottom of what's in that place. I'm going to call my mum and tell her she and Dad are going to have to drive out and take over. From Wednesday, my priority is the muster. That's what I came here for.'

'I was just thinking about that while Jon was outlining the program. George is a well-known and well-respected citizen of our area, and I know I could get a work crew together to help out. If you stay around for a while after the muster we can give you a hand if that helps.'

'That's a very kind offer, Kent. I'll give it some thought.'

'Like I said, the offer stands. He's a good old bloke. He was always the first one to help out anyone who needed a hand. I can still see him back in the 2012 floods. He wasn't a young man then, but he filled sandbags for days. And then when we were cut off for two weeks, he found an old tinnie in one of his sheds and organised food drops to the houses that were cut off.'

'It's so interesting to hear about him. I'm afraid I lost touch when I grew up, but I have memories of being out here when I was a kid.'

Fallon looked around as they entered the small yard at the back of the wide house surrounded by long shady verandas. The barbeque area was in a breezeway between two identically-sized sections and the young woman that she'd seen John speaking to at the pub the other night was standing with two of the small boys who were with Callie at the aerodrome.

Kent led her over to the young woman.

'Sophie this is Fallon Malone. She's our other helicopter pilot for the muster.'

'Hi, Fallon, good to meet you.' Her smile was sweet, but Sophie frowned as she flicked a glance at Kent.

Fallon looked over at him. His face was set and the friendly expression in his eyes had gone.

'Right, I'll go and see if I can help with the cooking.'

'It's all under control, Kent,' Sophie said.

'I'll go and get some beer then.' He started to walk away and then stopped.

Fallon noticed the tension in Sophie's stance.

'Fallon, don't leave before we have a chat. I want to talk about how we'll work things out on Wednesday.'

'Rightio,' she said.

Sophie rolled her eyes as Kent turned on his heel and headed back to the shed. 'Kent's a nice guy, but he overdoes it sometimes. He always makes me feel inadequate.'

Fallon shrugged. 'Always good to have someone who's willing to help out.' She wondered what their history was; there was obviously some tension between them. She looked up as Callie came out of the house carrying a tray.

'Hi again. I see you two have met. Soph, can you go and get your potato bake out of the oven, please? Nigel and Petie, go and find your brother and then the three of you can feed the pups and lock them away. Otherwise, the guys will feed them too many leftovers.'

The two boys ran off, and Sophie went inside.

'I haven't had potato bake for ages. Not since I left home. Mum used to make it,' Fallon said.

'Goes down a treat,' Callie said. 'Sophie is an amazing cook. She's going to move home now that she's back in the district, and I'm going to pick up another couple of days at the school.'

'At the school?'

'Yeah, I came out here as a nanny for the boys, but I've picked up some casual teaching. I told Braden now that Sophie's come back, he doesn't really need me here.'

Her face flushed pink.

'And?' Fallon asked with a grin.

'He wasn't impressed. We sat down and worked out a new salary. I refuse to be paid for helping out, now that we're together. He's going to try and hire a housekeeper. I said it wasn't fair that Sophie came back in and took all the responsibility.'

'You said Sophie is his sister?'

'Yeah. She had the boys for a couple of years after their mum was killed.' Callie lowered her voice. 'She's had a pretty tough time. Between you and me, I don't think she's happy with me being here. That's one of the reasons that I've tried to pull back a bit. I think she resents me being here. It's made things a bit awkward. But don't get me wrong. I'm really happy Kent and Braden went and got her.'

'I'm sure it'll all work out for you. People can be hard work. That's why I'm a loner.' One of the reasons anyway, Fallon thought.

'Anyway, I'm yakking too much,' Callie said. 'It's just good to have another pair of ears. So, how have you been going?'

Fallon filled Callie in on her progress and ignored Jon as he walked past them and headed over to the temporary bar.

'He's another really nice guy. They seem to breed them out here.' Callie's grin was wide.

'He's okay. Seems like a good boss.'

'But?' Callie asked.

'We had a bit of a shaky start.'

'We definitely need a coffee date. I'm working in town tomorrow, and the boys have footie training. Do you want to catch up?'

'Sounds good to me.' Fallon pointed to the bar. 'I think Kent needs you.'

'Okay, go and grab a plate. Some of the meat's already cooked and here's Sophie with the potato bake.'

Kent came over to where Fallon was sitting alone on the edge of the group. A couple of the stockmen had come up and introduced themselves, but Jon had stayed away.

Not that she expected him to babysit her, just because she'd followed him out here. But she couldn't help the little bit of disappointment that sat in her chest.

'So let's have a chat.' Kent held out a can of beer.

'Okay then. One won't hurt. I'm going to head off soon. I don't want to risk driving back in the dark. Too many roos out there and I'd be horrified if I hit one in Uncle George's car.'

'Bit late. They'll be on the move already.' Kent glanced across to where Callie and Sophie were manning the food table. 'Callie said she hoped you'd bunk down here for the night. This will turn into a bit of a do, and Jed has his guitar and his mate, Bobby, is a bit of a bush poet. Worth staying. They put on a good show.'

Fallon bit her lip. 'God, I'd never forgive myself if I hit a roo in his ute.'

'Think about it. Now I just want to get sorted with the way you operate. It's the first time I've done such a big muster out here. I usually just do my own.'

'I'm used to—' Fallon broke off as she encountered the hostile gaze of one of the stockmen who hadn't spoken to her yet. At the back of the area to the right of the large barbeque, a small bar had been set up. Half a dozen of the men sat there, beer cans in their hands. The man stared at her with a strange look on his face and when she held his eye for a moment, he frowned but didn't look away. It was the same guy who'd stared at her before when he'd been talking to Jon. He looked familiar but she couldn't put a name to his face or place him.

Chapter 9

'Will you camp out?'

Fallon turned her attention back to Kent as he asked her a few more questions.

'No, I'll drive back into town at night. I'm used to long distances. The only thing that worries me is driving George's vintage ute.'

'I'm sure Braden would lend you a farm ute.'

'I could take the chopper back to the aerodrome. I hope my ute'll be fixed in a few days.'

'Don't hold your breath. Jack Anderson's not known for his speed.'

'I'll have a think about it.' As she answered, Fallon was aware of the guy still staring. He watched her for a while longer and then turned to the man next to him and said something. The second man frowned and stared.

Fallon shrugged, just someone else who didn't want a female on the team. She'd encountered it before and didn't let it bother her as long as they stayed away from her and didn't cause trouble.

She gave her full attention to Kent as he continued. 'I'm sure I'll get used to working in a pair. I'm a bit of a worrier. I need to know exactly what's going to happen. It used to drive Sophie crazy.'

Fallon ignored the Sophie reference and chuckled. 'That's one thing we don't know when we're mustering from the air. And that's the thing I love about the job.'

'Mate, can you grab another carton from the shed?' Braden called out to Kent.

'Big drinkers, these guys,' Kent said as he stood. 'But Jon'll make sure they don't drink much out on the mustering camp. That's why he and Braden decided to put tonight on, plus there'll be another wind-up barbie after we're done.' Kent put his hand on her shoulder before he walked away. 'Thanks, Fallon. I'm looking forward to working with you. Now grab something to eat, before it all disappears.'

Along the middle of the breezeway, a table was loaded with paper plates, bread rolls, Sophie's potato bake, a big bowl of coleslaw, and a huge platter of meat.

'I wonder what the problem is,' Callie said as she came over to Fallon. Did something happen while I was inside?' She looked over at Jon and Braden who were heads-down talking outside the breezeway. They were both frowning

'No. I don't think so. I've been talking to Kent,' Fallon said.

'I'll be back in a minute. Get some dinner and I'll come and sit with you.'

Fallon picked up a bread roll and a small piece of steak, squirted tomato sauce on it and added a spoonful of coleslaw and potato bake. There were a couple of empty stools at the edge of the breezeway and she moved over and sat down—out of sight of the two guys who kept looking at her—staring out to the yard as she ate her bread roll. Braden's boys were playing on a structure at the back of the yard with three small pups running around them.

Everyone here seemed tense this afternoon, and she was keen to go back to town to the peace and quiet of the empty house. She'd drive slowly, put the lights on high beam and watch out for roos.

Even Callie wasn't her usual carefree self, and there was no sign of Sophie. Fallon put the second half of her bread roll down on the plate and dabbed at her mouth with the serviette. That was why she didn't have much to do with people. She didn't have time for all of this.

Doing her job, keeping to herself suited her just fine. Then when she was ready for a break, she'd head back to Cairns where she could go out on the water. One day when she'd saved enough, she'd move into her house there, and maybe do some flying over the reef with a tourist company.

Mum was always nagging her about being a loner but Fallon had never told her why. She'd never mentioned the incident eight years ago. Mum never read the news so she didn't know.

No matter what you did, people were judgemental and it was easier to stay away from them. Being alone was hard sometimes, and when she saw couples out together, looking happy, a small part of her wondered if she would ever find someone who understood her.

Suck it up, princess, she told herself.

She'd cry off the coffee date with Callie, and spend the time sorting George's house.

Her appetite gone, Fallon decided to head back to town. She stood and took the half-empty plate over to the large bin in the corner and dropped it in.

Jon was walking across to the bin as she turned. His face was set with deep lines grooved at each side of his mouth. 'Can I have a word, please?'

Fallon nodded. 'Is something wrong?'

He jerked his head rudely. 'Outside.'

***

Fallon's confidence and seeming self-sufficiency pissed Jon off. He was starting to regret that he'd listened to all the talk of how good she was and that he'd contracted her without an interview.

Now, he had more reason to worry about her suitability for the job.

He strode over to the shed and turned to gesture for her to follow.

That'd be right. She was lagging about twenty metres away behind him, and his temper fired. He stood, holding onto the door of the shed as he waited for her to walk over—at her pace—and when she stepped inside, he closed the door and flipped the lock over.

Her eyes widened and her lips were set in a straight line. 'Is that necessary?'

'I don't want to be interrupted. You have some explaining to do.'

She leaned back against the door and folded her arms.

God, she was annoyingly cool.

Ice Queen, not Chardonnay Girl.

He waited for her to speak, but not a word. Only a cool, hard stare.

'Why didn't you tell me you'd crashed a helicopter?'

Her face lost its colour and then a red spot appeared on each cheek. If it was possible, her lips tightened even more.

He waited her out, but she just stared at him.

'Well?' he said.

Still silence and his temper built.

'Look, Fallon, we need to sort this out. If I'd known you had a blemished record, I wouldn't have offered you the contract.'

She unfolded her arms and stood straight. 'And if I'd known it was *you* offering the contract, I wouldn't have signed it.'

'Why?'

'Because *you're* the one with the blemished record. Consider the contract rescinded, and may I suggest that next time you check your facts before you go making unfounded accusations. I'm sure there'll be some sort of clause in it that you can save face if you sack me but be prepared for a compensation claim from *Wyndham Birds*. There were plenty of other jobs that they knocked back to send me down here. Plus, I'm not prepared to work with a manager who treats me like you've treated me.'

As she stared at him with fire in her eyes, he saw the moment she realised who'd accused her.

'Ah, I knew I recognised his face. He was the ringer up at Barkly Roadhouse. So memorable I can't even remember his name.' Her laugh was bitter. 'He seems to like spreading his opinion far and wide. That was the same night I heard what a shit boss you were. I thought it was just nasty gossip or sour grapes but he got that bit right, didn't he? You're a bully and a smart arse.'

She pushed away from the door and turned to flick the lock over, but Jon stepped forward and put his hand on her arm.

'Wait. Don't go tearing off with the shits.'

'What? How dare you speak to me like that? And take your hand off me. I'm leaving here now, and I'm leaving town tomorrow. I don't have to take this from anyone.'

Jon dropped his hand. 'Wait, please. Are you telling me you didn't have an accident? He knew all about it.' He ran a hand through his hair in frustration. Braden had told him to simply ask Fallon what had happened; he hadn't jumped to a wild conclusion. He should have got Kent to talk to her. He always seemed to be able to keep the peace.

'Listen carefully. I have never crashed a bird. If I had I would have been up front with you this morning, especially knowing you were shit scared about being up in the air.'

'I wasn't.' He lied, but he hated the thought of his weakness being recognised.

'Whatever you say. You might be loose with the truth, but *I'm* not. I have *been* in a helicopter crash. Perhaps your informer needs to get his facts straight.' Her eyes were glacial, but he could see her hand shaking. She wasn't as cool as she was making out.

'Tell me about it.'

'Why?'

Because if I have been lied to, I'll apologise to you, and I'll deal with the person who lied to me.'

'How will you deal with him? Drag him over here and lock him in a shed while you tear strips off him? Or is that only something you do to women?'

'I wanted to give you privacy.'

'Bullshit, Jon. You wanted to give *you* power.'

'Talk to me, Fallon.'

'Why should I?'

'Because I want to know what happened. I'll put a stop to any misinformation that's being bandied about.'

***

Fallon cleared her throat and put a hand to her mouth as she coughed. Her mouth was dry from the shock of Jon's unfair accusation. Her temper had cooled. She was disappointed in him, but to be fair she could see where he was coming from.

'Maybe you'd better change the way you work, or you won't be here for very long,' she said. 'Get me a drink, and I'll tell you what you want to know.' No please, no pleasant tone.

Fallon had meant water, but when Jon came back from the fridge with a can of beer and popped the top open, she took it and drank deeply.

She walked away from him and crossed to the small table beside the fridge. She put the beer on the table, pulled the chair out and sat down. He followed her over and his expression was wary.

'Sit down, and don't look at me like that. I'm the one who's been treated badly here. What I'll tell you is the truth. I have no reason to lie. I'm not staying and you can Google it and check what I tell you anyway. Your source could have done that, but he obviously just wants to cause trouble.'

She sat straight and clenched her hands on her lap as Jon sat opposite her. 'I don't talk about this. It took me a long time to get over it. I had a year when I didn't fly. Yes, I was in a crash. The pilot died and I survived, and if you're wondering why I am so pedantic when I fly, now you know.'

'Even though I already had my licence and I asked my instructor to take me up one afternoon to show me something, I guess it was technically my fault.' She was determined not to break. Even though it had been Ken's role, the guilt of making the request to go up that afternoon had stayed with Fallon a long time, and she had shed many tears.

'Ken, my instructor, was a good man. He was married, his kids were grown up, and his first grandchild was on the way. He was the one who always told us over and over again about autorotation and not to go too low and to keep our speed up. I had been up with him a few times when he did it, and I'd had one go myself, but I wasn't confident enough to try it again without another lesson. I wanted to be sure.'

'What's autorotation mean?' Jon's voice held a note that hadn't been there before.

'If you're flying at five hundred feet or higher, and you have engine problems you've got a good chance of being able to auto-rotate out of any difficulty. If you have an airspeed of seventy nautical miles, you've also got a fairly good chance of a controlled crash.'

'What happened?'

She picked up the beer and drank again, and began to feel a little calmer, but her voice was flat. It was like being back in that investigation after the crash when she had to explain the technical side of the crash. 'During autorotation, the main rotor blades are driven by forces caused by the air coming from underneath as the machine descends. It's a misconception that choppers just fall from the sky. When we muster, we fly under three hundred feet and can go down to thirty miles per hour when we're after a beast or a stray herd. If your engine fails or you stall, you don't have any time to react, and you're too low to do it anyway. You just fall to the ground. Ken misjudged and we hit the ground.'

'Were you hurt?'

Fallon closed her eyes.

The noise and the smoke . . . she knew she had to get out. The sound and the impact of the machine hitting the ground thudded through her chest and her head. Something wet ran across her left eye and she blinked, and it hurt like hell. Like saltwater when she dived into the ocean.

'Ken!' she screamed. 'Get out. Get out.' The bird was on its side and she had to undo her belt and climb up and over the side. She jumped to the ground and ran around to the front, her head pounding. The windscreen was smashed and she could see her instructor and friend. As the darkness began to take over her vision and her knees collapsed, she knew it was too late. Sobs shook her body and the last thing she remembered was putting her fist against her teeth to stop the pain.

'Physically? No. A bit of a scratch here and there, and a mother of a headache and earache for a week or two. But hurt? Not really.'

'Emotionally?' he asked softly.

Fallon opened her eyes. *When did he get up?*

Jon was crouched in front of her and his hands were holding hers. She hadn't heard him move or felt his touch.

'What—' Her voice cracked and she swallowed. 'What do you think? I couldn't help him. When I came to, I'd been dragged away from the wreck but then I watched it burn. And my friend was inside.'

His hands tightened on hers, and he shook his head slowly from side to side. 'How the hell do you get back in and fly?'

'You heal. But you keep yourself safe. Safe from everything.' She pulled her hands from his. 'I need to go.'

Jon was still in front of her and he blocked her escape. 'I'm sorry, Fallon. I was out of line and I shouldn't have spoken to you like that because of what I was told.'

'You can check my story.'

'I won't be checking anything, and I sincerely hope that you'll accept my apology and reconsider.'

'Reconsider what?'

'Staying.'

She lifted her head and held that piercing blue gaze. 'Why should I?'

'Because I want you to.' She looked down as he took her hand again, and smoothed his thumb over the back of her hand. 'It's no excuse, but my inappropriate behaviour was a reaction to me fighting myself. And this will probably be enough to make you run, but I'm going to be honest. Ever since I walked into the pub yesterday and saw you sitting there, something happened.'

'Something like what?' The gentle pressure of his thumb soothed her, but a wave of tiredness washed over her.

'I never mix business with pleasure. But I haven't been able to get you out of my head. And that made me angry. Not with you, with myself, and I seized on what Rod said. Without thinking about it, and I was out of line, and for that, I'm truly sorry.'

Fallon put a hand to her head. 'I don't know. I'm too stressed to think about it right now.'

'And you're not in any fit state to drive.'

'I'm not.' She was with it enough to admit that. 'Will you go and get Callie, please? She said I could stay the night.'

'Good.' His voice was brisk and he pushed up to his feet. 'We'll talk in the morning when you're feeling better.'

'Maybe. I'll see how I feel.'

Chapter 10

Fallon rolled over and stretched her legs. The sheets were a lot softer than what she'd been sleeping in for the past few nights at Uncle George's, and the pillow was heaven. She lay on her back, opened her eyes and watched the ceiling fan spinning slowly above her.

Callie had been super kind last night. She'd taken her out of the back door of the shed and around the other side of the house and then walked her down to the donga. Once she'd checked Fallon was okay, she put a bottle of water beside the bed, and told her to sleep well.

The sun was streaming in through the sheer curtains. Fallon rolled over and picked up her phone, and sat up quickly when she saw it was past eight. Her clothes and boots were on the floor, and there was a towel and a pack of toiletries on the table near the bed.

Embarrassment flooded through her as she sat up and swung her legs to the floor. At least only Jon and Callie had seen her lose her shit last night. Callie didn't even know what had happened between them in the shed, but she'd looked after

109

Fallon, and made sure she was comfortable in the spare room of her donga.

Fallon didn't know what to do. The thought of facing Jon Ingram this morning—who she'd finally admitted to herself in the early hours, she was attracted to—was daunting. And *she* didn't mix business with pleasure either. She didn't even like him, so what was this feeling that consumed her?

Grabbing the towel, she headed for the tiny ensuite, vowing to put her embarrassment aside before she went outside. With a bit of luck, there'd be no one around and she could head back to town and decide what to do.

She stood under the hot water and quickly soaped her body, and then washed her hair, unsure of the water situation out here. She dried off, pulled her clothes on quickly, and finger-combed her hair. Then she pulled up the bed, picked up the water bottle and drank what was left. She dug in her pocket for the ute keys and was pleased to feel them beneath her fingers.

As she headed for the door, there was a tap on the other side. Expecting Callie, she put a smile on her face and pulled it open. Her smile faded and she took a quick step back as her gaze settled on Jon.

'Good morning,' he said. 'I was a bit worried you'd wake up early and head back to town, so I waited by your ute. Then I got worried when you *didn't* appear.'

'I don't run away,' she replied. 'I did that for too long.'

'Have you got any coffee in here? I've been waiting out by your ute since sun-up.'

'I don't know. I didn't look.'

'Will you? I'd kill for a coffee. And we can sit on your veranda and talk. There's no one around here. Callie's taken the kids to school, and I think Sophie must have gone with her. Braden and Kent have headed out to the camp with the stockmen ready for Wednesday.'

Fallon looked at him for a moment, ignoring the little jump of her heart, before she turned back into the donga and opened the cupboards in the small kitchenette.

To his credit, Jon waited outside.

'Come in, ' she said. 'You're in luck. There's some instant coffee and tea bags and long-life milk.' She lifted out the small plastic kettle and filled it at the tap. 'It won't compare with yesterday's coffee and Danish, but it's coffee.'

'Thank you.' Jon took his Akubra off and left it on the table on the veranda before he came in. 'Like you say, it's coffee. Did you sleep okay?'

'I did, thank you. Did you camp out?' Her voice was extremely polite.

'Slept in my swag next to my ute. I'm still staying at the pub in town. There's a manager's house at the back of the property I'll be moving into. Braden's getting it rewired. I lived there when I was here before, but it nearly burnt down, the power points were always catching fire, and the lights would work some nights and not others.'

Fallon put the coffee and milk into two cups and turned on the jug. She opened the fridge to put the opened carton of milk away and looked up at Jon.

'Would you like some toast? Callie's left some bread and butter and jam in here.'

'Only if you're having some.' His tone was as polite as hers, and Fallon was tempted to giggle.

She took the bread out and put two slices in the toaster on the bench. Although the atmosphere was so very civilised and tension-free, her hands were shaky and her heart was thudding.

When the jug boiled, she poured the water into the cups. The toast popped up, but Jon beat her to the cupboard and took out two plates. He quickly buttered the toast and added jam.

'One slice do you?' he asked.

'Is one enough for you?' she countered.

'Yes, one's fine.'

Fallon couldn't help the smile that tugged at her lips. 'We're being very polite. No Miss Chardonnay today.'

'I'm too scared to open my mouth apart from my pleases and thank yous,' he said. I'm scared of getting my head chopped off.'

His cute grin sent her heartbeat up to the next level, and she tried to feel cross at the effect he was having on her. Jon admitting last night that he was attracted to her had seemed to open something inside Fallon. She never had this reaction to a man.

Or if she had, it hadn't been for a very long time. It felt strange, but it wasn't scaring her.

Not too much.

'I'm pleased to hear that. Nice to see a bit of respect and manners.' Her tone was light and took any sting out of her words.

'Did you notice there's a veranda through that door?'

She looked at the door at the back of the donga he was pointing at. 'No. I didn't have time to explore.'

'Let's take our breakfast out there and sit. There's another table and chairs and a nice view over the dam.

When she nodded, Jon walked over and opened the door and then came back for his coffee and the plate of toast. He stood back and let her go outside first, and Fallon drew in a breath at the pretty sight.

A large dam shone blue under the clear sky, and in the distance, the western mountains picked up the morning sunlight.

'I feel at home out here,' he said. 'There's just something about the air and the landscape that's special.'

'Were you born out here? I mean is it your geographic home?'

'No, I was born on a station up on the Gulf. I grew up around cattle. My dad was the manager. When he died, Mum and I moved into Normanton, and I worked on a few different spreads up there. That's where I've worked most of my life.'

'How did you end up out here?'

So far their conversation was easy and tension free. It was as though they were two different people to the pair who'd gone head to head in the shed last night.

'I met Braden and Julia at a cattleman's conference in Longreach. He was looking for a manager and he offered me a good package.'

'And how long were you here for?'

'A couple of years. I was here when Nigel and Petie were born, but I'd gone before Julia's accident.'

'Is it okay to ask what happened? A car accident? I don't want to pry.'

114

'It's not prying. It's common knowledge. Julia was killed in a storm. The finding was accidental death. She was crushed by a horse.'

'Oh, how sad.'

'It was awful. I came down for the funeral. Sophie was incredible. She stepped in and took over looking after the boys. She grew up almost overnight.'

'You said you'd already gone by then. Did you decide to move on?'

For the first time, Jon seemed tense. 'No, family duty called.' He didn't elaborate, but she assumed it was to do with his mother.

Jon put his cup down and looked at her. 'Shall we talk about the elephant in the room?'

Fallon nodded. 'I accept your apology. I'm also sorry how I flared up too. I haven't talked about the crash for a long time, and it upset me.'

'That's fine. I was way out of line. I spoke to Rod last night and told him to pull his head in, and not gossip.'

'He wouldn't have taken that well.'

'He didn't. If he won't play by the rules, he can go.'

'Thank you. Now to put you out of your worry, I've decided to stay. I committed and I signed a contract.'

Fallon hid her smile as Jon's shoulders visibly relaxed.

'Thank you, Fallon. I really appreciate that. And I promise to be on my best behaviour for the whole muster.'

'It would leave you shorthanded if I went.'

He shook his head. 'We would have managed. But I'm really happy you're staying. I'd like to get to know you better. I meant what I said last night.'

'What about not mixing business and pleasure?' she asked as a little tug of happiness pulled inside her.

'Being friends isn't mixing business and pleasure.'

She nodded.

'And there's always weekends, and between musters to explore more.'

She looked at him, and something passed between them as she nodded again, and Jon smiled.

'You'll have to be very patient with me. I'm not good at friendship or anything else,' Fallon said.

'You and me both. I think we're both loners. We can learn together.'

Fallon leaned back and held his gaze. 'Can I trust you or is that a lady-killer pickup line? "We can learn together?" Learn what exactly?'

Jon put his head back and laughed. 'You've been listening to the town gossip, I'd say?'

'I have been warned. On several occasions.' She couldn't help smiling. 'So what's the go?'

'Apparently, it's because I break hearts when I refuse the offers of the local ladies.'

'It must be hard being a heartthrob.'

'Show a bit of respect, Fallon.' His grin was still wide. 'Okay, so what's your plan for today? You've got a day and a bit before the muster.'

'More house sorting out. And I might go and visit Uncle George.'

'Want some company?'

Surprise filled her. 'You don't have to. I thought you'd be busy out here?'

'I don't start officially until Wednesday. I just came out early to get things organised. So I've got some time up my sleeve. After seeing the outside of that house, I'd say you could do with a hand? Someone to help lift and carry?'

'I'm not going to knock back an offer like that. Thank you. Some company would be good, but I'll warn you. Poor old Uncle George's house is a bit depressing.'

Well then, let's get to town,' he said. 'I'll give you the day on a promise.'

'Oh?' Her eyebrows rose. 'On a promise? What sort of promise would that be?'

'If you ask me out to the pub for dinner, and feed me, I won't say no.'

'I can do that.'
'Well, Miss Chardonnay. Let's go to town.'

Chapter 11

Fallon

'How many casserole dishes does one man need?' Fallon sat on the kitchen floor and passed the last of two dozen casserole dishes up to Jon who was wrapping them and placing them in boxes on the countertop.

'Maybe they were wedding presents?' he offered.

'He never married.'

'Maybe they were his mother's?'

'Nope. They're seventies vintage. My mother has the same Corningware set. She just doesn't have dozens of them!' Fallon tapped her finger to her lips and then grimaced as she saw how dirty her hands were. She wiped her mouth with the back of her hand. 'Maybe he lived in sin? I had to take a box of stuff that had Josie's stuff in it to the aged care home in the middle of the night. I wondered who Josie was.'

'Maybe you could ask him when you visit him? He might like to talk about her if she was the love of his life.'

'He doesn't even know who I am. He's got dementia.'

'People with dementia will often respond if they're reminded of familiar things.'

'You sound as though you know about it.'

'Sadly, I do. That's why I had to leave here. To be close to my mum. It's a shocking disease.'

'I'm sorry to hear that. It makes me feel guilty that I get cross with my mum. I guess she only wants the best for me. I'm a pretty awful daughter.'

'I can't imagine that.' Jon held his hand out. 'Come on, I think you've done enough down there.'

She reached up and took his hand and looked down at his fingers before she stood. 'You have piano player's fingers.'

His cheeks flushed and Fallon pushed herself to her feet. Jon didn't let go and he tugged her hand so she was up against him as he leaned back on the kitchen bench. 'Don't you dare tell anyone, but Mum made me take piano lessons for that reason.'

Her smile spread wide. 'And do you still play?'

'I do, but I don't share that around. It doesn't go with the image.'

'What the lady-killer?'

'No.' He pulled her a little closer and she could feel his breath on her face as she looked up at him. 'The tough cattleman.'

'Well, I think—'

But Jon didn't wait to hear what she thought as his lips sought and found Fallon's.

***

Jon tangled his fingers in her short hair and his mouth was hard against hers. She opened her lips to him and he fell into the kiss, not wanting it to end. Kissing Fallon Malone reminded Jon of the time he'd been trampled on by a steer. When he came up for air, his chest hurt and he felt as though he couldn't breathe. His thoughts wouldn't settle and all he wanted to do was keep hold of her, and kiss her again, but Fallon pulled back.

'Whoa, boy,' she said, fanning herself with one dirty hand as something flickered in her eyes. 'I can see where your nickname came from. Lady-killer hits the mark.'

'Uh uh,' he said quietly. 'I haven't kissed anyone in this town.'

'As opposed to other towns?' she asked cheekily. He liked this Fallon.

Very much.

Way too much.

He didn't want to break her heart. A heart that he knew was already damaged.

But he couldn't help himself.

Her skin was warm against him and he lowered his mouth to her neck, caressing her skin with his lips. The sigh that warmed his skin spoke volumes and he knew exactly what she was feeling.

Finally, she pulled back and stepped away from him, but he could see the rate her chest was rising and falling. Her eyes were huge as she stared at him. 'If that's friendship, I don't know if I could cope with more.'

'We'll just have to take it as it comes. Unless you'd rather I left?'

He was pleased with her instant head shake and smiled at her words.

'No, you're too handy in the kitchen.'

'It's getting late. Are you going to visit your uncle? Then you have to take me for that promised pub meal.'

Her back was to him and her voice was hesitant as she crossed to the sink and washed her hands. 'Would you like to come with me? He might talk to a man?'

Jon hesitated. He wasn't going to admit to his weakness. 'You go. I've got a few calls to make, and then I'll have a shower and walk back and pick you up.'

'Walk back? So you can drive the ute again?'

'No. I thought we might have a bottle of wine with dinner. Make it a real date while we're off duty.'

'Okay. I'll go and clean up and visit him. What time will you come back?'

'Six okay?'

She nodded but stayed over the other side of the kitchen. 'Okay, just pull the door shut on your way out.' She disappeared up the hall before he could answer and Jon wondered if he'd upset her.

***

'Hello, young Sally. About time you came to see me.' Great-Uncle George's eyes were bright and lucid, and his smile was wide. He was clean-shaven and his hair was neatly combed.

'Hello, Uncle George You're looking very dapper today.'

He leaned forward and whispered, 'I got them to clean me up. Josie's coming to see me.'

'Is she?' Fallon widened her eyes. *The mysterious Josie.* 'Does she live in town?'

'Of course, she does. She lives in our house. Where else would she be?' His voice began to get agitated. 'She's late. Did you tell her to stay at home?'

'No, of course not.' Fallon searched desperately for something to say. 'Um, I went to the butcher and got that meat for Sooty yesterday.'

'What butcher? Who's Sooty? What are you talking about you stupid girl? You're the one who took my pink box. I want it. Go and get it. It's under the bed.' His voice turned into a full-blown roar. 'Now!'

The aide came hurrying into the TV room where they were sitting, and stood in front of George. 'Now what's the problem here? Have you had your cup of tea, George?

'I don't want a bloody cup of tea. I want Josie to come. She can take me home, away from all you bitches.' He stood up and his chair tipped over as he lunged for Fallon. As she took a step back, two male aides came hurrying and each took one of George's arms.

'Come on, mate, we'll go for a walk in the garden.'

'Is Josie out there?' Suddenly his voice was docile. Fallon blinked back tears as a hard lump formed in her throat.

'Let's go and see.'

'Sorry, love, but you seem to set him off. Maybe it's best to stay away until we get his medication sorted out.'

'Medication?'

'The doctor has prescribed some anti-psychotic drugs and we're trying to get the dose sorted.'

'Why would he be on anti-psychotic drugs?'

'Don't be upset, love. We called your mother. She's the only contact we have. People with some forms of dementia can get aggressive and disruptive. They believe things that aren't true. And the more confused they are, the worse it can be.

They can be a risk to themselves, and to other residents and staff, so the medication is pretty much essential.'

'That's sad.'

'Life's cruel. And we see it all in here. I'll give your mum a call and let her know what's going on. I'll call her when it's okay for you to come back for a visit.'

'Thank you.' Fallon's light and happy mood after spending the day with Jon plummeted. 'What was the point of cleaning out George's house? He'd never go back there, and it didn't matter what happened to everything in it.

As Fallon walked through town back to the house, she pulled out her phone and dialled home. It answered straight away.

'Fallon. Where are you? Have you started work yet? How's the house going?'

'Hi, Mum. I'm still at Augathella and that would be a no, and a yes. I've just been to see Uncle George. He's not good, Mum.'

'I know, sweetie. We're going to try and get out there, but there's always so much happening here. I'm on so many committees, I'm always needed.'

'You're needed here, Mum. *I* need you, too.'

There was silence at the other end of the phone for a while. 'That's lovely to hear you say that. I thought you didn't need us these days.'

'Well, I do, and it's probably a long time since I told you and Dad I love you. It would be good to see you. If you don't come out here, I'll come home after this contract is done.'

'That would be really good.' Her mother's voice was thick with emotion. 'And you know how much Dad and I love you too. We miss you so much, Fallon.'

Fallon cleared her throat. 'I have to go. I'm going out for dinner at the pub soon, but I just wanted to ask you if you had ever heard of a Josie? Uncle George is fixated on her visiting him.'

'Oh no, the poor dear. He must be losing it.'

'Why? Who was she?'

'Apparently, they got engaged before he went to Vietnam. She was a local girl, and she was killed in a road accident while he was overseas. I think it was after that he let the house go. He lost interest in everything.'

'That is sad. Anyway, Mum, I've done a couple of rooms, and I've got one more day left before I start work on Wednesday. I'll probably be out of touch if you're trying to call me, but you can leave a message at *Kilcoy Station* if you need me. I'll text you the number.'

'Thanks, love. Now you be careful up there. Don't go taking any risks, will you?'

'No, Mum. I never do.'

'Okay, we'll talk soon, and don't get yourself upset about George. It's sad, but he's a very old man. Love you, darling.'

'Love you too, Mum. Bye.'

Fallon blinked back tears as she walked along the footpaths. George might be an old man, but once he'd been young like she was. He'd had hopes and dreams, and his dreams had been dashed and he'd obviously never recovered.

It's a wake-up call for me, she thought. *I've buried myself away alone for too long. It's time to start living my life before it's too late.*

Fallon took a deep breath and quickened her pace, her lips lifting in a smile as a plan formed in her head.

Chapter 12

Jon whistled as he did the buttons up on his dress shirt. He'd even got the ironing board out of the cupboard in his hotel room and pressed his shirt and jeans. A quick shower, a flick of the comb and a splash of the aftershave he'd bought at the local pharmacy, and he was ready to walk to the house and pick Fallon up for dinner. Guilt had stayed with him for a while; he'd sensed that Fallon would have liked company at the aged care home when she'd visited George, but he couldn't do it. The memories of those last few months with Mum in the home at Normanton were deeply buried and that's where he wanted them to stay. He knew if he had gone there with her, the smells, the vacant stares, and the cheery staff would have brought it all back.

The months she had been in there had been awful. Mum had been too young; she hadn't even reached seventy.

Jon pushed away the sad thoughts and took one final look in the mirror.

'You'll do, mate,' he said to his reflection. He couldn't believe he was going on a date, and with one of his team, but he'd fallen under Fallon's spell.

She fascinated him; she was tough and sassy, but she was also gentle and vulnerable.

On the way down through the main part of the pub, he stopped at the bistro to book a table. Being a Monday night, he didn't think it would be busy, but he'd hate to have to take Fallon to the local fish and chip shop instead. To his surprise, Sophie was behind the counter.

'Soph? What are you doing here?'

Sophie's eyes were shadowed as she looked up from the napkins she was folding, but she gave Jon a smile. 'I'm working. Took a part-time job in town to get out of Braden and Callie's hair. They don't need me there every night. What are you doing? You're all dressed up.'

'I wanted to book a table. Although it doesn't look too busy.'

'It's going to be. We've got a busload of tourists arriving in half an hour. The bistro is full.'

'Damn.' Jon pulled a face.

'It's okay. Sean's opened the dining room tonight because the Rotary committee wanted dinner before their meeting, and we've got some other locals coming in.' She picked up a pen. 'How many and what time?'

'Two and in about half an hour. Maybe a corner table? Private?'

Her grin was cheeky. 'On a date, hey? Not like you to be out with the locals, Mr Lady-killer. Now you're a local again, you'll change your tune?'

Jon's face heated. 'She's not a local.'

'Hmm. interesting. I'm in the bistro tonight, but I'll make sure you get looked after.'

'Thanks, Soph. You're a sweetheart. How are you, anyway?'

'I'm okay. I've settled back in at *Kilcoy Station*, although it's funny being back at home. I know I made a wrong choice with Jock, and it was silly to move so far away, but it's all over now and I'll get over it.'

'Good. If you ever need a big brother's ear, just call me.'

She chuckled. 'Yeah, Braden's busy. Having the boys back and then hooking up with Callie, and the muster coming up, he doesn't have much spare time.'

'Callie seems nice. Do you reckon she'll stay?'

'I'd be shocked if she left. They're really good for each other. She's fitted in really well for a city chick. And the boys love her already.'

'I'm happy for them. Okay, be back soon.'

'I'm looking forward to seeing your date.'

'Be good.' He lifted his hand in a wave as he headed out.

***

Fallon glanced at her watch as she added a few drops of water to the mascara tube. It had been so long since she'd worn makeup it was dry and hard. She'd been pleased when she found lipstick and mascara in the bottom of her toiletries bag. The long floral dress she always carried in her bag was wrinkle-free and with a squirt of perfume had lost the musty smell from being packed away for a long time. The only problem was shoes, but once she'd given her boots a lick of polish, they sort of looked trendy with the calf-length dress. She'd washed her hair, and finger-dried it after searching for a hairdryer with no luck.

Butterflies danced in Fallon's stomach as she sat at the kitchen table—the clean kitchen table—and pulled out her phone. She was ready way too early. She flicked through her emails, read a couple of newsletters and managed to get her nerves under control.

God, that kiss. She hadn't been kissed so thoroughly for a long time.

If ever.

Had she made a mistake responding to him? Not that she'd done it consciously. Plus, was she too ready to trust Jon after he'd thought the worst of her yesterday?

Logic told her she was making a mistake. Her emotions, hormones, and heart told her she wasn't.

What would be, would be. And she'd be gone from here in three weeks or so, and there was nothing wrong with enjoying herself while she was here. It would be a first to let go and spend some time with someone else.

She sat up straight in the chair. Or was she making too much of an assumption?

God, why were relationships so hard? She pulled herself up. No. it wasn't a relationship. A friendship.

Tingles ran through her nerve endings as she thought of Jon's mouth exploring hers. Friendship didn't feel like that.

God, maybe she should just cancel. She tensed as footsteps came up the back path and a shadow fell across the back door.

'Come in,' she called as she stood and waited.

Chapter 13

Sophie

Sophie reached for the next pile of napkins waiting to be folded. What she'd told Jon about taking a job in town to give Braden and Callie some space, well, it hadn't been the exact truth. The problem was, she couldn't stand the sympathetic looks and the quiet that fell when she walked into the room.

She felt like standing there and screaming, 'I made a mistake, but I'm all right!'

But of course, she didn't. She went to her old room; the room that Julia had always insisted was hers, and lay on the bed thinking of the mistakes she'd made.

Okay, so she'd been the one who'd made the wrong choice, and the stupid mistake, and taken everything Jock had said as the truth.

We'll move away and we'll have a fresh start together, Soph.

Your brother doesn't like me. He wants to control you.

Yeah sure, Jock. Who had been the control freak? And she had fallen for it, thinking it was love.

I only want the best for you, Sophie, so that's not a good idea.

You need to get away from those kids. You're too young to be at their beck and call.

And the big one?

Once we get settled in the north, we'll start our own family.

But once Jock had her away from her familiar surroundings, and Braden's support, he'd changed. He'd shown his true colours, and she knew she had been an absolute fool.

The first time he'd hit her after a few beers had been an accident, he'd said.

The second time brought her to her senses and she called Braden. There wasn't going to be a third time. She'd driven to the small town of Ravenshoe and waited for Braden to arrive.

The worst thing of all was the embarrassment about Kent being involved with her "rescue". He'd been kind, but aloof, and she knew he was the one who judged her for her poor choice, and the stupid mistake she'd made.

The times the boys had said that Uncle Jock had been cruel to them, she'd taken it as being strict. She hadn't realised it had been physical cruelty, and she had been sick to the stomach when she'd discovered that.

'Sophie?'

Her head flew up and the napkins scattered on the floor as she met the gaze of one of the men she'd been thinking about. Heat flooded her cheeks as she met Kent Mason's steady gaze, and she knew he'd notice. He knew her well. Too well.

'Kent. I didn't hear you come in. How can I help you?'

'I assume you're working here?' he said, looking at the unfolded napkins on the counter next to her.

'No. I was just walking past and saw the napkins needed folding.' Sarcasm laced her words.

'Sweet of you.' His voice was clipped. 'Are you taking the reservations?'

'I am. When for?'

'Tonight. I heard the bistro is closed so I thought I'd better book the dining room.'

'Why? Has everyone heard I'm working tonight and wants to have a gander?'

Kent's eyes were cold. 'Actually no. My friends and I would like to have a meal. It's not all—' He cut off his words.

'It's not all about you, Sophie,' she finished for him sweetly. She knew Kent well enough to know what he'd been going to say.

'If it fits.' He raised his broad shoulders in a shrug.

'Oh, it fits. You're such an expert on me. You know exactly what a selfish bitch I am.'

The sigh that came from him hurt more than his words. All she was to Kent these days was nuisance value. An exasperation. Someone who'd created a situation so he'd had to fly her brother almost a thousand kilometres to rescue her from a situation of her making.

'How many and what time?' She just wanted him to go away.

'Four of us for seven o'clock please.'

'Do you have a table preference?'

'No.'

'Done.' She picked up the next napkin and started folding it.

Sean, the chef, came out of the kitchen and stood a little too close to her for comfort. Sophie stepped away from him a little.

'Did I hear some more bookings come in?' he asked.

'Yes, another six. It's going to be a busy night. That's ten tables in the dining room now.'

'Who's waitressing in the dining room.'

Sean frowned. 'You are.'

'So who's in the bistro?'

He looked at her. 'You are.'

'What by myself? Both? A busload of oldies in here, and ten tables in the dining room. I can't do that.'

'You'll have to. We've got no other staff. It's Maggie's night off and she's out of town.'

'I'd better go and set the tables then. I thought I was in here.'

'Get your skates on.'

Sophie started to panic. She'd had a couple of nights in the bistro, but she had no idea how the dining room worked. She'd never even waitressed before.

Take a deep breath. How hard can it be to ask someone what they want to eat? Take it to the kitchen and bring it back out.

Not rocket science.

She raced into the dining room, pleased to see that the tables already had clean tablecloths on them. And the cutlery was in an obvious place on the antique sideboard. She and Braden had come here for Sunday lunch when they were kids with Mum and Dad when they were still alive.

All she had to do was remember to set the table properly.

An hour later, Sophie was feeling a lot calmer. The bus passengers in the bistro had a set menu and all she had to do was carry the meals out and they swapped the meals around the table to whoever wanted chicken or steak. Once they were all served she smoothed her hair back and picked up a pen and the order pad.

Three of the tables in the dining room were full, and the customers had bought their drinks at the bar. Kent's party hadn't arrived yet, and she was surprised to see Jon already sitting at the table in the corner with Fallon, the new helicopter pilot. They must have come in when she was in the kitchen. She picked up two menus and walked over to them.

Well, well, well. Sophie hid her surprise when she noticed Jon holding Fallon's hand on top of the table. As she approached, Fallon moved her hand and put it in her lap.

Sophie looked down at the menus pretending she hadn't noticed.

'Hi, Jon. Hi, Fallon. Looks like you guys are right for drinks?'

A wine bottle sat in a cooler bucket on the table and their glasses were filled with white wine.

'Hello, Sophie,' Fallon said.

Sophie almost did a double-take. The new helicopter pilot looked drop-dead gorgeous. A pretty colourful floral dress with a sweetheart neckline, a touch of makeup and a pretty pink lipstick; Fallon looked totally different to the woman in the high vis shirt Sophie had met the other day at the station.

She handed Fallon a menu and reached for the napkin to put in her lap, but Fallon shook her head. 'No need to do all that.'

Sophie smiled and repeated what Sean had told her. 'There's only the menu tonight. No specials board, because the bistro is full.'

'That's fine,' Jon said. 'Don't worry about us too much. We'll be right.' The look in his eyes as he looked at Fallon surprised Sophie. Looked like the fancy dress and the makeup had woven a spell on Jon. As long as Fallon didn't hurt him, Sophie thought. Jon was a decent guy.

She looked from one to the other and was surprised to see a similar expression on Fallon's face.

Even more interesting.

'I'll be back to get your order in a little while.'

Sophie smiled when Jon reached up and squeezed her hand. 'You're doing great, Soph. Good to see you home again.'

She turned to go to the next table and froze when she noticed Kent, Bob Hamblin, the state school principal and his wife, and another woman—drop-dead gorgeous, of course—waiting at the door.

She plastered a smile on her face, picked up four menus off the sideboard and greeted them.

'Hello, Kent. Hi Bob, Cheryl. Please follow me, and I'll get you seated.' As they sat she waited for Kent to introduce the woman she didn't know, and then realised she was the waitress and didn't warrant an introduction.

She stood behind the unfamiliar woman and a cloud of musky perfume hit her nostrils as she flicked the napkin onto her lap.

Not even a thank you or a nod. She shoved the four menus in the middle of the table and said, 'I'll be back in fifteen minutes to take your order.'

'We'd like some drinks while we choose,' the perfumed woman said.

Sophie couldn't help herself. 'Bar's that way.' She gestured with her head and moved on to the small Rotary group at the next table. 'Would you like another drink while you wait for your entrées, Dan?' she almost whispered.

'Thanks, Sophie.' Dan, the president winked at her. 'We'll go to the bar too. You've got the Probus Club out there to deal with.'

'The what?'

'Your bus group.'

'Ah. Okay. I didn't know what they were.'

Sophie headed for the kitchen and ignored Kent's table. She frowned. Why was she letting them bother her?'

***

A little shiver ran down Fallon's back as Jon took her hand and they stepped out onto the street. Dinner had been wonderful. The food, the wine, the service, and most of all, the company. They'd both opened up to each other and Jon had told her about the rough few years looking after his mum.

Fallon felt as though they'd been friends for a long time. They were quiet, each lost in their own thoughts as they walked down past the shops to the corner that led to George's house. She wondered what sort of day George had had after she left.

'I wonder how George is going?' Jon commented as they passed the aged care home.

'Mind reader,' she said. 'I was just thinking that.'

'I'm sorry I didn't go with you today.'

She shook her head. 'After hearing what you and your mum went through, I don't expect you to. I probably won't go back again. It just upsets him. Besides, we'll be busy soon.'

They were quiet again as they walked through the silent streets, and it wasn't long before they were at the back door of George's house. Sooty was sitting outside meowing.

'Does he want to go inside?'

'He's got a secret entry that I haven't found yet. But no, he wants food. I swear he hadn't eaten before I found him in there. It's all he does.'

Jon held out his hand for the key when Fallon took it out of her bag. She hesitated when he opened the door, and then came to the decision that she'd been stewing over all night. Life was too short to wait for what you wanted. She took a deep breath and met his gaze.

'Would you like to come in?' she asked.

Chapter 14

'Get outa there,' Jon yelled as the lumbering black beast headed for a small stand of trees between the stockmen and the boundary fence. The noise of Fallon's helicopter above filled the air, and he didn't want her to have to come down lower. He'd been worried about that ever since she'd explained that auto stuff to him last week.

To his relief, the beast turned as Rod and his offsider galloped in behind it and got it back on track. The taciturn stockman had been even quieter since Jon had had a word to him, but the gossip had stopped. Less than six days after they'd started the muster on Braden's place, the last of the cattle were heading for the yards.

His headset crackled and Kent's words were loud.

'We'll head back to my place. Okay with that?'

'All good. Ask Fallon to ring me if she wants me to pick her up.' Fallon had left George's ute in town, and hers was still at the garage.

'You're hopeless, mate. I've never seen a man fall so hard and fast. Then again, Braden was nearly as quick when Callie turned up.'

Jon grinned and looked up as the two choppers banked to the east back to Kent's property where Fallon's machine had spent the past week or so. 'Your turn next,' he said.

'Nope. Confirmed bachelor here, mate.'

'I'll catch you for a beer somewhere later,' Jon said.

'Over and out.'

The speed at which his relationship with Fallon had developed made Jon very happy. He had no doubt that moving in together was right. They'd been inseparable since the first night he'd stayed at her place. After a couple of nights together in her single bed, they'd headed out to stay at the manager's residence at the back of Braden's property. The house came with Job's contract and had been recently renovated. The rewiring had been completed, so he had no fear of them being burned in their bed. Sooty had moved out with them and was proving to be a champion mouser. A couple of days ago Callie brought the boys and their puppies out, and Sooty had kept them all in line.

Jon hadn't felt this contented for a long time, and he knew he had a goofy grin on his face as he cantered after the stockmen. He pushed away the thought of Fallon living after the muster; he'd do everything he could to convince her to stay.

The noise of the helicopters receded and the only noise was the occasional snort of a beast and thudding hooves as the stragglers were herded into the yard.

Jon caught up to Braden as they went back to camp. The horses would stay out here, and he'd take Braden back to the house.

'A successful week,' his boss said as they headed along the road. 'Let's hope Kent's and Craig's go as well. Who's next?'

'Craig's place,' Jon said. 'Thought we'd get the furthest one out of the way. Kent's should be easier too. We're going to keep going and start tomorrow seeing we're ahead.'

'Do you need me?'

'No, we'll be right. They're a good team.'

'And so are Fallon and Kent. What're the chances of getting her to stay out this way or am I asking too soon?'

'If I had my way, it would be a given. I'll be doing my best to convince her.'

'Won't take much. I've seen the way you pair are together. You might be a fast mover, Jon, but I think she's as smitten as you are.

Jon grinned. 'I hope so.'

'And if she goes, will you follow?'

'To be honest, mate? I'd have to think about it. I know it might seem fast, but I'll do whatever it takes—' Jon shrugged. 'I'm not going to let her get away.'

'Good on you. She's a good person. She and Callie have really hit it off too. Plus it'd be good to have two helicopter pilots out here.'

'I'll see what I can do.'

***

Fallon waited for Jon to come and get her at Kent's big shed.

They both leaned back on the fence and sipped on the cold bottled water that Kent had brought out.

'Thanks, I needed that.' Fallon wiped the back of her hand over her mouth. 'It was hot out there today.'

'Good job, though. You're an excellent pilot, Fallon. Made me feel rusty. I should do more flying, but there's always so much to do at my place.' He shot her a sideways glance. 'We need a pilot out this way.'

'Do you?' She stared at him. 'Is there a hidden meaning there?'

'Take it how you want. I know someone who'd be very happy if you stayed.'

'Do you?'

Fallon's stomach was unsettled. The more she thought about leaving here when the last muster was done, the more she wondered what she wanted.

No, she knew what she wanted—she wanted to stay with Jon. But she couldn't very well say to him, *I'm leaving my job and moving in.*

It was just the first excitement of a new romance.

And regular sex. She couldn't hold back the grin that tugged at her mouth.

'And by the grin on your face, you do too.'

'Do what?'

'Know who wants you to stay.'

'Because he needs a pilot?'

'That too.'

Fallon shrugged. 'I've got a job, and I've got commitments. But the time it's taking to fix my ute I could still be here at Christmas!'

'No one would mind.'

Jon was quiet when he picked her up and they took the back road home.

Home. Had a nice ring to it, but it was too soon.

Wasn't it?

'A big day for you. Tired?' she said finally. 'You're quiet.'

'Yeah, a bit, but it's great to be done ahead of schedule.' He reached over and squeezed her hand. 'And you and Kent did good. You work well together. It certainly sped up the process. You got those cattle moving well. Best I've seen.'

'I enjoyed it.'

'I've been thinking about Craig's place. We didn't fly over it last week, and now he wants to use the other yards, I think I should go up with you tomorrow morning. I want to be sure you know the route. Kent's busy in the morning and I'd like you to see how close the cattle are to the channels. If they get spooked we'd be in all sorts of trouble. And once we lose them, you know how hard it is to get them back on track.'

'Okay. Sounds like a plan. Would you like me to cook tonight?'

'How about we do it together? I'll barbeque and you can do some veggies.'

'I can do that.'

'I'd like to have a drink first though. There's something I want to run by you.'

Fallon's stomach sank at the same time a ripple of excitement began. She wondered what he was going to talk about, and what she would say if he asked what Kent had suggested.

Chapter 15

Jon poured a white wine for Fallon and grabbed a beer for himself. They'd kept their drinks to only one a night as they were both aware of the big days they'd had ahead of them over the past ten days. They sat on the small porch that faced west and watched the sun sink behind the low mountain range.

'It's really pretty here,' Fallon murmured. Jon glanced over at her; she sounded half asleep. Maybe this wasn't the time to bring up his idea. Or was it a proposition? Or a proposal? He sat up straight and almost spilled his beer. A proposal, now that was an idea.

'Did you know this is where Braden and Sophie grew up?'

'I wondered. It was the original house on the station?'

'Yeah. Apparently, their parents were in their forties when they had the kids, and they've both been gone for a few years. Braden moved the location and built the big house when he got married.'

'Life goes so quickly, doesn't it? Seeing George and his house of old stuff really bothered me. Made me think.'

Jon moved his chair closer to Fallon's and took her hand in his. 'I've been thinking too. You might think I'm crazy, and I don't know how to say this, so I'll come right out and say it.'

His heart sank when Fallon pulled her hand away from his.

'Please don't. Please don't spoil it.'

'Hear me out? Please?'

Fallon sighed and waited.

'I don't want you to go, Fallon. I know everyone would say it's way too soon for any sort of commitment. Hell, other people who've known each other the short two weeks we have, would probably only be on their second date. I know it's too soon for the L-word, but honestly, I just want you to stay. The thought of you leaving and going so far away is awful.'

He waited while she put her head back and closed her eyes. Her face was pale and looked tired and he worried about the pressure he was putting on her.

'I love being here, and I really care about you, Jon, but it's too soon to be talking about leaving everything I know.'

'Can I cut to the chase? How important is "everything you know" to you?'

She shrugged. 'I don't know. It's familiar and it's safe.'

'I can be safe for you.'

'What if this flame dies down? What if I gave up my life and came here and then you realised it was the wrong thing. You wouldn't be able to tell me because I'd be here. I know I'm not making sense, but you want me to give up my life on a two-week fling?'

'It's more than a fling to me,' he said quietly. 'I've never felt like this before, and if I have to pull out the L-word, I'll use it.'

'Don't "pull" it out. Just let me go home, and we'll keep in touch and we'll see what happens.'

'I know what will happen. We'll both be busy with our lives with things that don't matter, and it'll be too hard. Fallon, I'm not prepared to risk that. Are you?'

When he finally found the courage to look at her, he saw the answer in her eyes, and his heart broke.

'Okay, I'll go and heat up the barbie. You put the veggies on.' Jon walked through the kitchen, took a second beer from the fridge and went out to the back deck. He stood, his hands grasping the railing as he realised he'd blown it.

***

Fallon barely slept, and when she and Jon drove to Kent's shed the following morning to take her helicopter up over Craig's station, her eyes were gritty and her stomach was roiling. She'd been sick every morning for the past week, and a horrible thought was niggling at her. She couldn't be pregnant surely? It was way too soon to get sick. Not that she knew much about it. She must have eaten something. Or it was the tank water? Or stress that was playing up with her? Her digestion was always the first thing to go when she was worried about something.

She'd gone as far as Googling early symptoms and it *was* possible. Strangely, the thought didn't spook her; she knew Jon well enough to know that he'd be happy too. He'd held her in his arms this morning, and for the first time, she doubted her decision to leave, but she told herself it was too soon. If it was meant to be—what a stupid term that was—they would keep seeing each other despite being three thousand kilometres apart.

Unless she *was* pregnant; then it would be a whole different ball game.

Yep, she'd looked on Google maps last night. Three thousand bloody kilometres. It might as well be to the moon and back.

Kent seemed to be in a bad mood too when they arrived at the shed.

'I'm in a bit of a rush. I have to go into town first up. Is there anything you need?' he asked, tapping his fingers on the side of his thigh.

'If you have time, and only if you do, could you call into Jack Anderson's garage and see if my ute is anywhere near ready?' Fallon asked. 'I haven't talked to him since before the muster.'

'I can do that.' He turned towards his ute. 'I'll give you a call later.'

'Thanks.' Fallon crossed to the helicopter and pulled her phone out. She hadn't even checked the forecast this morning. Too much on her mind.

'Damn,' she muttered.

'What's wrong?' Jon was staring past her towards the horizon, his face pale. His mood was no better than hers or Kent's, and she knew he wouldn't want to go up.

'No service here. I didn't check the weather.'

He pointed to the sky. 'No wind. No clouds and we won't be up long. Ten minutes out and then ten back.'

'Okay, jump in. I'll do the safety check and we'll be off.'

When she'd finished, and climbed in and passed him the headset. Jon had his head back and his eyes were closed.

'You okay?' she asked.

'I'll live. Let's get going.'

'North?' Fallon asked.

'North.' He nodded and slipped the headset on and closed his eyes again.

A small spurt of anger tugged at Fallon. *Men!* What was it about them that they had the right to be cross, but she didn't?

Okay, he was upset, but so was she. She wasn't sure if she was making the right choice, and she hadn't slept all night as she'd worried over the pros and cons of staying or leaving. She wondered how George was going, and she was worried about her ute and how much it was going to cost.

She checked that Jon was buckled up, and pressed the starter. As soon as the throb of the motor vibrated through the machine, she began to feel better, as flying took over her thoughts and not all those niggling worries.

Her nose was tickling, and she put her hand up as she sneezed.

Jon opened his eyes and glanced over. 'Not getting a cold are you?'

'No. It's the dry air.' She sneezed again and her eyes burned.

God, that was all she needed today. A head cold.

'My throat's a bit scratchy too. I hope I haven't shared any germs with you,' came through her headset.

She flicked him a grin as her mood improved slightly. 'Bit late for that.'

At least she got a smile in return.

Jon leaned forward and pointed ahead. 'That's Craig's southern yards. Bear west about ten degrees and we'll get to his boundary where the main yards are.'

'There's a lot of cattle down there.'

'Yeah, he runs more than Braden and Kent. This is going to be the biggest muster of the three.'

Fallon changed direction as Jon indicated. Ahead to the northwest, the water of the channel country glinted in the morning sun.

'Ah, I see them. There's a few utes and swags down there already.'

'Yeah, some of the ringers came out and set up camp yesterday afternoon. Some went back to town too.'

'Okay, I've sussed it out enough now.' Fallon nodded.

'Most of the cattle are back the way we came so you'll be flying into the sun in the afternoons. Will that be safe?'

'Yes, Jon, it will be safe.'

Fallon moved the cyclic stick connected to the central column located between the two seats, to put the bird into a left roll to head back to Kent's station.

'Kent seemed a bit stressed this morning, did you think?' she said.

'Didn't notice. Probably worrying about the muster on his place.' He looked over at her. 'And Sophie.'

'Sophie?' She frowned as they began to turn back.

'Yeah, I didn't know but apparently they were a couple for a long time before her ex came on the scene. Kent was muttering to Braden about her the other day. Braden told me afterwards she was rude to the people Kent was having dinner with the night we were there for dinner.'

'I didn't notice.'

His voice was low. 'I don't think either of us noticed much that night.'

'True.'

The helicopter slewed sideways as a strong gust of wind came from nowhere. Fallon increased their airspeed and moved the nose up. She looked ahead with a frown. 'Jon, what's that ahead?'

He lifted his head and peered forward. 'How fast can we get back?'

'Why?'

'That's a mother of a dust storm coming.'

'And there'll be wind with it.' Fallon scanned the horizon. 'It's only a few kilometres wide. We're not going to outrun it, so I'm going to head north. I think we'll be able to avoid the worst of it that way. I should have checked the forecast.' She cursed herself for being slack and letting her worries overtake her usual safety procedures. 'I'm sorry, Jon. My fault. Tighten your belt.'

'I'm fine. I have every faith in your skill, Fallon.' His voice was calm.

'We're just going to have to go the long way home.' Fallon nodded. 'If it gets too close, we'll land and let it pass. Won't be pleasant if we have to sit it out.'

'You mean if the wind's strong?'

'Yes, I'd rather outrun it, because we won't have time or somewhere to tie it down,'

'What about Craig's place? The homestead I mean.'

'Which way is it.'

'Back towards the storm.'

'No, too much of a risk. We'll be fine. Look you can see the edge of it to the northwest.' Fallon didn't express her fear that the wind would be more widespread than the dust storm.

As they headed north, Fallon sneezed again. The sky darkened and she frowned. The storm was getting too close, too fast and they weren't going to outrun it. She looked down, but it was hard to see below the dust that was starting to swirl beneath them.

She kept her tone even as the wind began to buffet the chopper. 'I'm going to take her down. Do you know what's beneath us?'

'Channel country.'

'And that is?'

'Salt pans, salt lakes, lots of water, and some ground.' Jon grabbed for the side of his seat as another strong gust pushed the bird sideways and the first of the dust hit them. Almost immediately the auxiliary power cut as dust was sucked in through the intakes.

'Brace position, Jon. I'm going into autorotate.' Fallon focused on her breathing, drawing the air in deep and letting it out slowly. It was impossible to see the ground and the first rule of a safe landing was clear pilot vision.

Jon leaned forward. 'What about you?'

'I'm flying.' She barely heard him as she focused in the helicopter.

'I love you, Fallon.' He crossed his arms in front of his head.

Her heart lodged in her throat.

I can do this. After Ken had died eight years ago, she'd gone straight up and taken herself through an autorotation. Now, the dust shrouded them as the engine cut out completely. The whoosh of the air from the spinning rotors and the dust grinding on the windscreen were the only sounds. Fallon tensed, fighting to control the bird in the descent without an engine.

She pulled back on the cyclic and the main rotor blades picked up speed as she desperately tried to work out how high they were. Levelling off, she pulled up on the collective and stared through the side door. The windscreen was covered with brown dust. As she brought the chopper lower, a flash of water glinted through the dust briefly. They didn't want a water landing. She pulled back to slow her forward speed and glanced across past Jon. There was an expanse of green directly ahead of them; Drawing in another breath, she levelled the helicopter.

Five metres to go.

'Come on, Fallon,' she whispered as the grass loomed ahead. 'Do this for Ken.'

Her control held as the chopper got closer to the ground. 'We're almost there, Jon.'

The chopper flipped sideways in one swift movement as the skids sank into something soft on one side. The seatbelt held her pinned against the seat as water sprayed around them. Jon's head ricocheted off the metal door beside her as the machine tipped over to his side. His eyes were closed.

'Jon, are you okay?' she screamed.

There was no answer.

Chapter 16

Kent

Kent was having an early lunch at the coffee shop with Jennifer, the new school counsellor at the state school. She was working across Augathella, Tambo, and Charleville schools and had said it would be good to learn more about the district. He tried his best to get out of it at dinner the other night—saying not having kids at the school, he wasn't much help—but he hadn't been able to fob her off without sounding churlish. He'd somehow let her know today this was a one off. He wasn't available to drop everything and come to town for lunch.

He hadn't known that Bob and Cheryl were bringing Jennifer to dinner last week until Cheryl had rung up and asked him to book for four. It *had* been satisfying to see Sophie's reaction. It showed her he wasn't spending his life waiting for her to decide she was ready to pick up with him again.

Oh no. He'd had his heart broken by Sophie once, and he was in full self-protection mode now.

Jennifer was sitting at a table under the awning of The Hot Pot, the local coffee shop. She was dressed in a business suit, and heavily made-up, her perfume overpowering. Kent felt out of place, he'd headed off in his work clothes and he brushed the dust off his trousers as he walked over.

'Hello, Jennifer,' he said, trying to give her a friendly smile that didn't hold an invitation. To his horror, she grabbed his arm and planted a kiss on his cheek.

'Hello, Kent, it's *so* good to see you again.'

He nodded. 'Have you ordered?'

'No. I was hoping we might go to the pub again when I finish my coffee. I've had a really difficult morning, and I could do with a glass of wine.'

Kent resisted the inclination to raise his eyebrows. 'Sorry Jennifer, I've only got half an hour.'

She sighed. 'Okay, next time I'm doing an overnighter here we'll go out for dinner by ourselves.'

Will we? he thought. *I don't think so.* But he said, 'I can't stay long. We're in the middle of mustering and I have to get back to the station.'

She put a manicured hand to her head and patted her perfect hair. 'God, yes. This horrid child. Nigel Cartwright, he threw a chair at me.'

'Ah, isn't that confidential?'

She ignored him and her words rushed on. 'Okay. His mum might have died, and he might be upset, but how dare he do that?'

'It's understandable.' Kent was horrified at her lack of confidentiality and consideration for the poor kid, but he wasn't going to let on he knew the family.

'No, it's not.'

'Have you had grief training?' he couldn't resist asking.

'No. I'm a primary teacher and I've enrolled in a psychology degree under a training program because they can't get counsellors out west. Anyway, enough about me, Kent. Tell me about your station. Is it huge?'

Kent couldn't believe it when she literally fluttered her eyelashes. Before he could speak, a very familiar voice came from behind him.

'Hello, Kent. Unusual to see you in town at this time of day.'

He turned slowly, and sure enough, Sophie was standing behind him, dressed in her waitressing clothes.

'Hi, Soph. Working the lunchtime shift too, are you? I'm impressed.'

She nodded and waited, looking at Jennifer. Finally, she broke the awkward silence. 'Hello, I'm Sophie Cartwright.'

Jennifer flinched.

Kent's manners kicked back in. 'Sophie, this is Jennifer, she's the new counsellor at the school.'

'Ah.' Her eyes narrowed. 'My brother was telling me about you last night. You upset Nigel last time you were here.'

'And he upset *me* this morning!'

Sophie pursed her lips and Kent waited for it; he knew her well.

'Who's the grown-up?' she asked, putting her hands on her hips.

'I am.' Jennifer's voice was shrill. 'No child has the right to throw a chair at the teacher!'

'Even if that teacher told him Mummy was never coming back and he had to suck it up?'

Kent drew in a horrified breath. 'You didn't say that to Nigel, did you?'

'I'm afraid that's confidential.' Jennifer examined her perfect fingernails.

'And what were you doing seeing him today? You weren't supposed to see him again. Braden emailed a complaint to Bob.' Sophie had her hands on her hips now.

Jennifer shrugged, and Kent disliked her intensely at that moment. He stood and pushed his chair in. 'I'm sorry to be rude, Jenny, but I've got to go to the produce store and get back out to the station.'

'It's Jennifer.'

'Sorry, Jennifer. I hope your day improves.' He lifted his hand in a wave and turned to Sophie.

'Soph, I'll walk you to the pub.' He was surprised when Sophie nodded and slipped her hand through the crook of his elbow. The feel of her fingers even through his shirt brought back too many memories.

'What a cow,' she said loudly as they walked away. 'No one treats our boys like that and gets away with it. I'll be talking to Bob when I knock off at two.'

'Yeah, I agree,' he said as they approached the pub.

'I'm surprised to see you in town with that storm coming.' Once they turned the corner towards the pub, she removed her hand.

'Storm, what storm?' He looked up at the clear blue sky. There wasn't a breath of wind.

'There's a big dust storm rolling in. I rang Braden and told him I'd keep the boys in town at Aunty Rowena's place.'

'What about Callie?'

'She's off sick with a sore throat. I drove the boys in. Probably the dust.'

'Are you sure there's a storm?'

Sophie pulled a face and marched him across the road and up the slight hill behind the hotel. 'Look, I hope your girlfriend's not driving far this afternoon.'

'She's not my girlfriend and bloody hell, look at that. I'd better get home.' A huge, high rolling cloud of red and brown dust ran along the horizon as far as he could see north and south. It was the highest dust storm he'd seen for a long time and it was approaching fast. 'Shit, Jon and Fallon are flying in that.'

'What do you mean? In a helicopter?'

'Yes, they were heading out to Craig Wilson's place to look at the cattle yards.'

'When they saw that coming they would have turned around.' Sophie frowned and stared at the sky. Kent looked away; he found it hard to look at her since they'd broken up. It bought back too many memories.

'It's moving fast, so there must be a strong wind up high. I don't think they would have had time. I'll go to the SES and see if I can pick Fallon up on the radio. She might have put down out there.'

'Call Craig too, he might know. Maybe they stopped at the station.'

'Good idea. Thanks, Soph, I'll see you later.' His mind focused on Fallon and Jon, and out of years of habit, Kent leaned across and went to kiss her, but stopped when he realised what he was doing. He froze and cleared his throat. 'Okay. You take care.'

'You be careful too.' Her hand on his cheek as she lifted it almost brought him undone, and he moved back.

'I will. See you later.'

Kent didn't look back as he headed for his ute.

His head was full of Sophie as he climbed in and slammed the ute into gear, heading for the SES headquarters out near the aerodrome.

Chapter 17

Braden

Braden reached for his mobile as it rang for the fourth time in the last half hour. Sophie had rung to tell him about the storm heading to town and how she'd take the kids to Aunt Rowena's. That had made him feel guilty. Since Julia's death, he'd lost touch with their two aunts in town, but Sophie always kept in touch.

'Braden Cartwright,' he said, his attention on the spreadsheet on the computer.

'Bray, it's Kent. Would Jon and Fallon happen to be out there?'

Braden frowned. 'I don't think so. I haven't seen them since last night. What's wrong?'

'There's a huge dust storm rolling in and they flew out to Craig's place a couple of hours ago. I rang my place, but they haven't come back there and that's where Jon's ute is.'

'You think they're caught in it?'

'I hope not, but I can't raise Fallon on the radio.'

'Maybe they put it down at Craig's place when they saw it coming?'

'I got onto Craig and they're not there. He heard them go over a couple of hours ago.'

'What do you want me to do?'

'Not a lot we can do until this storm passes. It's just hit town. Won't be long before it reaches you. Just give me a buzz if they turn up. When the wind drops and it's clear, I'll take my chopper out.'

'Okay, keep me posted.'

'Will do.'

Braden saved his file, closed the laptop and headed to the kitchen. He'd told Callie to have an easy day seeing she'd felt too crook to go to school, but she said she was feeling better and headed to the kitchen to cook and freeze some meals, as well as make biscuits for the boys.

He stood in the doorway and watched her as she pulled a tray of biscuits from the oven and put them on the sink. Callie reached up and as she tucked a strand of stray hair back, she saw him. A sweet smile spread over her face as he walked over and put his arms around her.

'I thought you were working,' she said.

'I thought you were going to have a rest,' he countered.

'I feel fine now. My headache's gone, and my throat's back to normal.'

'It was probably the dust storm,' he said.

She leaned around him and looked out the window over the sink. 'What dust storm?'

'It's just hit town. Sophie rang, and then Kent. He's worried that Fallon and Jon are out that way in the helicopter.'

'I hope not. That one I was in at Mitchell was awful. Really scary, and I was inside a motel unit.'

'They are scary. Kent's going to keep an eye out for them. I think you should sleep in the house tonight.'

'Do you just?' she said with a cheeky grin.

'Well, I'll be lonely because the boys and Sophie are staying in town.'

'Hmm,' she said leaning into him. 'Not just because you want to have your wicked way with the nanny?'

'No, I'd like to have my wicked way with *my* woman,' he said brushing his lips over hers.

She chuckled. 'How about you help me clean up the kitchen and we'll have a—'

'A what?'

'A sleep?'

As Braden loaded the dishwasher and Callie covered the trays of biscuits, he kept his voice casual. 'I've been thinking.'

'Dangerous occupation, that,' she replied. 'Sorry.' She glanced at him as he came over to her. 'What have you been thinking?'

'I've been thinking it would be good if you moved into the house.'

She shook her head, and Braden put his hands on her shoulders. 'Hear me out, Callie?'

'Okay. What are you thinking?'

'Well, we're a couple now, aren't we?'

'I guess you could call us that.'

'The boys adore you and they hate you being over there at night in that small donga.'

'Do they?' She smiled.

'And so do I. It keeps me awake at nights.'

'Isn't it too soon? What would people say?'

'People like who?'

'Sophie?'

'No, my sister got stuck into me the other night and said it was about time you moved into the house. And although it's not the main reason, it's another reason. I think if Sophie could stay in the dongas, she'd come home more.'

'But this is her home.'

'It is to me. To us, but she lived at Jock's place for a couple of years before they moved north. I know she feels as though she's imposing. I even suggested that we open up the other side of the house.'

Callie lifted her hands and cupped his cheeks. 'That's a big step for you.'

'I need to take some big steps, Callie. I want to take a very big step.' He knew his voice was gruff. 'It's past time I cleaned out Julia's things, and we made full use of the house. Sophie said she'd help me but she won't move in there. So I want to suggest she has the donga. What do you think?'

His heart lightened when Callie finally nodded. 'Okay, I will, but on one condition.'

He raised his eyebrows. 'What condition?'

'As long as I have my own room. I'm not moving into your room. A small step first.'

'I can live with small steps.' Braden lowered his voice. 'As long as I can visit sometimes.'

Callie nodded, and he took her hand.

'Where are we going?'

'I thought we could take the opportunity to help you pick a bed? There's a few to choose from.'

'Lead the way,' she said with a sexy smile.

Chapter 18

Fallon wedged herself between Jon and the cockpit door on the other side of his seat and pushed as hard as she could but the door wouldn't budge. The chopper was on its side and the bottom of the door was buried in the soft mud.

Tendrils of panic wound their way through her limbs as she thought about fire. The tank had been almost full and she could smell aviation fuel. The chopper was on its side and as well as fire, she worried about it sinking, not knowing how deep the channels were out here.

Jon was out cold, but breathing normally, and his pulse was steady. There was no blood, but he had an egg-sized lump near his temple where his head had hit the metal when she'd brought the chopper down.

Frantic, she called his name trying to wake him up as she scrambled back over him and reached up to push her door open with both hands. It was hard at this angle, but finally, it moved and flipped over and hit the side of the machine.

'Jon, wake up. Please. we have to get out. We have to get out *now*.'

He muttered, and finally, his eyes fluttered open.

'Thank God.' Fallon tugged at his hands. 'I've undone your belt but you're going to have to help me. We have to get out fast.'

The chopper rocked as she managed to get him half to his feet, but he flopped back onto the seat. 'Can't. Dizzy.'

'You have to.'

Somehow, with a strength she didn't know she had, Fallon managed to push Jon up to her door. He leaned through it and she draped his arms over the top of the opening as he rested there with his eyes shut.

'I think I'm going to spew, Fallon.' At least he was talking and he knew who she was.

'That's okay, just do what you have to. But after we get you out.' She climbed over him and swung herself to the ground. She could just reach his hands and she tugged until he started to move with her.

After several long minutes of pulling and encouraging him, Jon was on the ground beside her. To her relief, this side of the machine was on solid ground. As the dust storm swirled around them, it was impossible to see more than a few metres ahead of them. She put her arm around Jon's waist and he leaned on her as they moved away from the chopper. The ground was soft beneath their feet and it wasn't long before their boots were sodden.

'Snakes,' he muttered. 'Bad out here.'

'Thanks for that,' she puffed out. 'Just what we need.' It wasn't long before they reached a piece of hard ground, far enough away from the chopper that if it did blow, they were safe.

Fallon helped Jon sit down, and she sat beside him. 'Lean on me, Jon. I'll look after you.'

He hadn't been sick, and he seemed to be waking more each minute. 'Should be looking after you,' he said.

Tears pricked at Fallon's eyes. They had come so close to death. It was a miracle that they had survived the crash from that height, but she'd be a lot happier once they got medical help. Jon had been out to it for too long.

She rested her cheek against his and closed her eyes. Even after knowing him for such a short time, she knew every inch of his face. The contours of his cheeks, his long eyelashes and the way he looked at her were familiar to her now, and she knew she couldn't walk away.

But this wasn't the time to tell him that.

'Jon,' she said as the wind roared around them, and dust stung their faces. 'Do you have your phone in your pocket?'

'In my hip pocket.'

Fallon reached down and he leaned over so she could get it out. As the screen lit up, relief surged through her as three bars of service showed at the top.

***

'I don't need to be admitted,' Jon complained. 'I just want to go home and sleep it off.'

Once the storm had settled it was only fifteen minutes until Kent's helicopter had hovered above them, and Fallon had directed him down to the wide expanse of solid ground about fifty metres from where she'd left Jon.

The doctor finally agreed to let Jon go on the condition that they stayed in town for the night, and he agreed begrudgingly.

'Just watch him through the night, Fallon. Keep waking him up and checking his eyes. If there are any problems, I'll send him to Charleville tomorrow for a scan.'

'I'm fine,' Jon insisted.

As they settled into the room that he'd had at the pub until a few weeks ago, Fallon sat on the bed beside him.

'If you're going to be a difficult patient, I might have to reconsider.' Her voice shook as the moments before the crash flashed through her mind.

'Reconsider? Reconsider what?'

'Staying out here. Not going back north.'

Jon's eyes crinkled and his lips tilted up in a huge smile. 'Really? You're really going to stay? Really and truly?'

'If you'll have me after I almost killed you.'

'It wasn't your fault.'

'It was. If I'd checked the forecast, we wouldn't have gone up.'

'Didn't you hear what Kent said?'

'No?' She shook her head.

'The storm only formed about a hundred ks west of Augathella and there was no mention of it on the forecast until it hit. So we would have still gone.'

Fallon's shoulders sagged in relief. 'That will stand me in good stead in the investigation. I'd hate to lose my licence.'

Jon sat up slowly and pulled Fallon into his arms. Her head rested on his shoulder and she absorbed the feel of his warm skin against hers.

'Do you know how happy you've made me?'

'I know. I haven't ever felt like this before either.'

'You know if you'd decided to go, I was going to follow you. I'd already discussed it with Braden.'

Fallon smiled as she lifted her head. 'There's a downside for you.'

'I can't think of one.'

'You get to help me clean out Uncle George's house.'

'Aha,' Jon said as his lips brushed the top of her head. 'But I also get to drive his ute too.'

'Maybe we could buy it off him? We might need it.'

' Need it?'

'Well, my ute's a single cab, and I have a little suspicion that I might need a bigger car, sooner rather than later.'

'You can drive the RAM anytime you need it, you know.' Jon leaned back and frowned. 'What for, moving stuff from the house?'

'Um no. Maybe for a baby seat. But only maybe. I *think* I could be pregnant.'

Fallon hadn't known that Jon's smile could get any wider.

Epilogue

'You've done an amazing job out here, love.'

Fallon smiled as she led her mother through Uncle George's house. Four weeks had passed since the crash, and those four weeks had been busy. Mum had arrived by plane earlier this afternoon, and Fallon had driven to Charleville to pick her up.

'Thanks, Mum. Jon and I spent a lot of time sorting out here after the musters were done.'

Fallon didn't see the need to tell her mother about the crash—after all, no one had been hurt, and there wasn't going to be an investigation. The dust storm had been accepted as the cause, and her boss from *Wyndham Birds* had flown down and told her how well she'd done to bring it down.

'I can't wait to meet your Jon. He must be pretty special if you're giving up your job to move down here.'

'He is. Very special.'

'Do you want to live here in George's house? I'm sure it would be fine.'

'No, we'll stay out on the station Jon's managing. Do you want to stay here while you're visiting? Or do you want to come out to our place?

Or the rooms at the pub are nice. Whatever you want to do, we'll fit in.'

'I think I'd like to stay here,' her mother said. 'I can walk up and see George every day, potter around and sort out the things you've put aside, and maybe you could take me out to the station for a visit?'

'And how about I stay here with you for a few nights and we can have a really good catch up? I've got lots of news.'

'And a wedding to plan?'

Fallon held out her hand and her engagement ring sparkled in the late afternoon sunlight streaming through the now-clean kitchen window.

'Yes. And a wedding to plan. But a small one. Just our local friends here, and you and Dad, if you can get him out here.'

'He'll be here. I've given him the date already.'

Fallon smiled as her mother's eyes settled on the cane pram Fallon had spent the last two weeks cleaning and relining. 'Oh and I've got another date for you, Mum. I'd love it if you'd come out when the baby arrives.'

Jon was walking in the front door when he heard the happy scream from the kitchen, and he knew exactly what had happened. He'd been feeling that way ever since Fallon's pregnancy test had been positive. He followed the noise down the hall to the kitchen where Fallon and a woman he assumed was her mother were both crying and laughing at the same time.

Fallon caught his eye over her mother's head, as they both wiped their eyes.

'Jon, this is my Mum, Ruth. Mum, this is Jon.'

'Hello, Ruth, it's great to finally meet you.' He leaned forward and kissed her cheek before he put his arm around Fallon and kissed her soundly.

'I've booked a table in the dining room. Callie and Braden and the boys are coming into town, and Kent's going to meet us there.'

'And Sophie?'

'Sophie's waitressing tonight.'

Fallon and Jon exchanged a smile. The whole town was waiting for Kent and Sophie to get back together.

'Come on, ladies.' Jon crooked both arms. 'I'll be the talk of the town with a pretty woman on each arm.'

Mum looked at Fallon and nodded. 'He's a keeper, love.'

Fallon smiled. 'He's a lady-killer.'

UNTIL THE NEXT STORY...

Callie, Fallon and Sophie's stories continue in *Outback Escape* as we learn more about those who live in the district.

When Sophie Cartwright comes home to Augathella, she doesn't get the welcome she expected. Her brother, Braden, has got his father act together, the new staff at *Kilcoy Station* are keeping things running, and Sophie, well, she feels . . . unwanted. As for her ex, Kent Mason, he and his attitude could go take a flying leap.

Kent Mason is cautious when Sophie comes home to *Kilcoy Station*. Maybe she'd finally grown up enough to make better life choices. He didn't have the time to worry about her anymore, and he wasn't prepared to be hurt again.

So how was it that they seemed to end up in each other's company more than ever?

The Augathella Girls series.

Book 1: Outback Roads -The Nanny

Book 2: Outback Sky -The Pilot

Book 3: Outback Escape – The Sister

Book 4: Outback Winds – The Jillaroo

Book 5: Outback Dawn – The Visitor

Book 6: Outback Moonlight – The Rogue

Book 7: Outback Dust – The Drifter

Book 8: Outback Hope – The Farmer

If you would like to stay up to date with Annie's releases, subscribe to her newsletter here: **http://www.annieseaton.net**

OTHER BOOKS from ANNIE

Whitsunday Dawn
Undara
Osprey Reef
East of Alice (2022)

Porter Sisters Series

Kakadu Sunset

Daintree

Diamond Sky

Hidden Valley

Larapinta

Pentecost Island Series

Pippa

Eliza

Nell

Tamsin

Evie

Cherry

Odessa

ANNIE SEATON

Sienna

Tess

Isla

The Augathella Girls Series (2022)

Outback Roads

Outback Skies

Outback Escape (June)

Plus more to follow

Sunshine Coast Series

Waiting for Ana

The Trouble with Jack

Healing His Heart

Sunshine Coast Boxed Set

The Richards Brothers Series

The Trouble with Paradise

Marry in Haste

Outback Sunrise

OUTBACK SKY

Bondi Beach Love Series

Beach House

Beach Music

Beach Walk

Beach Dreams

The House on the Hill

Second Chance Bay Series

Her Outback Playboy

Her Outback Protector

Her Outback Haven

Her Outback Paradise

*The McDougalls of Second Chance Bay
Boxed Set*

Love Across Time Series

Come Back to Me

Follow Me

Finding Home

The Threads that Bind

Others

ANNIE SEATON

Deadly Secrets

Adventures in Time

Silver Valley Witch

The Emerald Necklace

Worth the Wait

Ten Days in Paradise

Her Christmas Star

An Aussie Christmas Duo

Secrets of River Cottage (Nov)

About the Author

Annie lives in Australia, on the beautiful north coast of New South Wales. She sits in her writing chair and looks out over the tranquil Pacific Ocean.

She writes contemporary romance and loves telling stories that always have a happily ever after. She lives with her very own hero of many years and they share their home with Toby, the naughtiest dog in the universe, and Barney, the ragdoll puss, who hides when the four grandchildren come to visit.

Stay up to date with her latest releases at her website: **http://www.annieseaton.net**

9 780645 438192